MAR 15

Ting Ting

Kristie Hammond

WINLAW, BRITISH COLUMBIA

LIBRARY AND ARCHIVES CANADA CATALOGUING IN PUBLICATION
Hammond, Kristie, 1957-, author
    Ting Ting / Kristie Hammond.

ISBN 978-1-55039-210-4 (pbk.)

    I. Title.

PS8615.A5444T56 2013   JC813'.6   C2013-901978-2

This book is a work of fiction. Names, characters, places, and incidents are either the product of the author's imagination or are used fictitiously.

Sono Nis Press most gratefully acknowledges support for our publishing program provided by the Government of Canada through the Canada Book Fund and the Canada Council for the Arts, and by the Province of British Columbia through the British Columbia Arts Council and the Book Publishing Tax Credit, Ministry of Provincial Revenue.

Edited by Laura Peetoom
Copy edited by Dawn Loewen
Proofread by Audrey McClellan
Cover and interior design by Frances Hunter
Cover and frontispiece art by Aileen Kamonzeki

Published by
Sono Nis Press
Box 160
Winlaw, BC V0G 2J0
1-800-370-5228

Distributed in the U.S. by
Orca Book Publishers
Box 468
Custer, WA 98240-0468
1-800-210-5277

books@sononis.com
www.sononis.com

The Canada Council | Le Conseil des Arts
   for the Arts | du Canada

Printed and bound in Canada by Houghton Boston Printing.
Printed on acid-free paper that is forest friendly (100% post-consumer recycled paper) and has been processed chlorine free.

To my mom,

who can tell a story

better than anyone I know.

And to the memory of my dad.

I so wish you had been

here to read this.

Ting is a fictional character, but she was inspired by a real-life person. Like the Ting you are about to read about, the real-life Ting is also from Jinan, in Shandong Province, China. Her father left China to study in Canada, and her mother went to visit him right before the events of Tiananmen Square in the spring of 1989. Afterwards, her parents made the difficult decision to remain in Canada. Ting stayed with her aunt until she was eventually able to join her parents. And just like the character in the book, the real-life Ting has a lot of spunk and determination. Having said all of that, it is important to know that the people and events in this story, other than historical facts such as the Tiananmen Square protests, are all fictional. So while it is true this story was inspired by a real person, it is not a factual record of her story.

This book uses some Chinese (Mandarin) words, written with our alphabet in a form called pinyin. Mostly these are family words like *mama* (mother), *baba* (father), *yima* (aunt), and *yifu* (uncle). Although proper Chinese pronunciation is very tricky, you can think of these words as being pronounced roughly as you would guess. Some other words are harder to guess at. Here is a rough guide to pronouncing them:

laoye (mother's father—the maternal grandfather):
    lao yeh (*lao* rhymes with *now*)

laolao (mother's mother—the maternal grandmother): rhymes with *now now*

nainai (father's mother—the paternal grandmother):
    nye nye (*nye* rhymes with *eye*)

yeye (father's father—the paternal grandfather):
    yeh yeh

ni hao (hello):
    nee how

Qingdao (a city):
    ching dow

weiqi (game):
    way chee

xie xie (thank you):
    ssee-uh ssee-uh (*ssee* is pronounced partway between *see* and *she*)

yang rou chuan (meat on a skewer):
    young roh choo-ann

· Chapter 1 ·

Ting grabbed her mother's hand, pulling her along the crowded sidewalk toward the street vendor selling stick candy. It was Ting's favourite treat, but not one Mama would often buy her. She said too much stick candy would make Ting's teeth rot and fall out. This warning would always be accompanied by Mama saying, "That is what happened to Yeye's teeth, and now he can only eat congee."

When Ting was younger, these words scared her enough that she would stop begging her mama for the sweet treat, but now that she was eight years old she no longer believed the candy would make her teeth fall out. She had come to this conclusion after her grandfather saw her eating some one day and said, "I never did like stick candy, even when I was a little boy." She knew then that surely this could not have been what made Yeye's teeth fall out, although just to be on the safe side Ting was extra careful about brushing her teeth after the last glob was eaten off the sticks.

Ting now sat working the taffy, twirling and pulling it between the wooden skewers in an effort to turn it into the creamy mass that was just right to eat. She thought about how strange it was that today, when she asked Mama if they could go to Wu Street to see if the stick candy vendor had his stall set up, the usual words did not come out of her mama's mouth. In fact, she didn't really appear to be listening to Ting at all. She just nodded her head in a distracted way and told Ting to grab her jacket because it was cold outside. Stranger still was the fact that instead of going directly home afterwards, Mama said they needed to take the city bus to a building in another area of Jinan.

Bus rides weren't something Ting got to do very often, as they cost too much money. Like everyone else around them, the Li family's two main modes of transportation were their feet and their bicycles. Stick candy *and* a bus ride in one day seemed almost too good to be true, but not wanting to risk having Mama change her mind, Ting didn't ask any questions. When they finally arrived at their stop, Mama hurried Ting off the bus, grabbed her hand, and began pulling her to get her to go faster.

"Mama! My candy!" With only one of Ting's hands holding the two sticks, the now almost milky-white blob of candy was in danger of falling to the ground.

"If I let go of your hand, you must promise me you will keep up."

"Yes, Mama, I will. I promise."

It turned out it was not an easy promise to keep, as Ting's shorter legs had a hard time keeping up with her mama's long, hurried strides. Just when she thought she could not go one more step, Mama came to an abrupt halt in front of a tall grey building. There were several soldiers standing in front of the building, and Mama had to show them some papers before they would let her in. Once they got inside, there were many more soldiers and officials. A woman wearing a black skirt and plain white blouse ushered them into a waiting room filled with worried-looking people, some old, some young, some in families, some by themselves.

"Mama, where are we?" Ting asked in a quiet voice.

"Never mind. I will tell you later. Right now you must sit quietly and not go anywhere. When they call my name you stay here in your seat, and when I'm finished I will come to get you." Seeing the worried look on her daughter's face, her voice softened. "If you do as I say, we will buy a watermelon on the way home."

Ting loved watermelon more than any other fruit. When she was sick, she would beg her parents to buy her one. She told her parents that the fruit had magical healing powers. She knew it really had no such powers, it just plain tasted good, and when her throat was aching it was so easy to swallow. When she was burning up with a fever, each bite seemed to cool her down a little more. So the offer of watermelon was enough to make her an obedient daughter, but it did not stop the questions about the strange events of the day from swirling around in her mind.

· Chapter 2 ·

Ting usually liked having her aunts come to visit, especially Mei Yima. In her mama's family there were three girls. Ting's mama, Shu, was sandwiched between her older sister, Mei, and her younger sister, Bo. In typical fashion, the eldest sister tended to boss the other two around, still bossing even now that they were all grown women with families of their own. Though her words could sometimes be sharp, Ting knew Mei Yima had a soft heart. Many times she had seen her comfort a friend or a neighbour's crying baby, hand a coin to a beggar on the street, or, best of all, put an extra dumpling on Ting's plate during the New Year's celebrations.

Bo Yima was as quiet and timid as Mei Yima was outspoken. However, when she *did* speak, it was as if she measured every word, and the listener paid extra attention because of it. Often when Mama and Mei Yima were in the midst of a heated discussion, Bo Yima would speak a few soft words and the other two would look at her in surprise, then suddenly laugh, and all would be well again.

Now the women gathered around the table with

their cups of steaming hot green tea while Ting sat, seemingly intent on doing her schoolwork. This was a trick she had learned long ago. If she sat quietly and appeared to be occupied with some activity or other, they soon forgot about her and spoke freely. She had learned many interesting things this way. Sometimes they were small things, like why the couple in the house behind them were fighting, or who had just purchased a new television set. And sometimes they were big things, like who was getting married or what they thought about the latest government policies. (Ting always had to strain to hear any discussions about the government because voices got very quiet when talking about this dangerous subject.)

This was how Ting first heard that her father had been chosen to go to Canada as a visiting scholar. It wasn't until two weeks after her eavesdropping that her parents finally told her that Baba would be going away for two years to study, and that it was an honour for him to have been chosen to represent his country. It had been difficult for her to pretend to be surprised when she heard the news, but she knew she must try or Mama would become suspicious. All of that had happened several months ago. Ting missed her baba very much, but she didn't have time to think about that right now. She was too busy concentrating on what her yimas and Mama were saying.

Voices were getting louder as the discussion around the table went on, which wasn't in itself unusual. What was different this time was whose voice was growing stronger—Bo Yima's.

"This is craziness! You cannot travel to Canada all by yourself. Think of Ting Ting."

At the mention of Ting's nickname, her yimas and Mama quickly looked over at her to see if she had heard. Ting hunched over her notebook with her pen in hand, making broad strokes on the page, apparently fully absorbed. Satisfied that she was not paying attention, they continued their conversation. It was Bo Yima again, although her voice was back to its usual quiet calmness.

"Li Hai can come back here if he is missing you so much. It's too much to ask to have you pay so much money to go visit him in this far-off country."

"You know he cannot return before his exchange time is up, or the government will be very upset with him," said Shu, giving her younger sister a disapproving glare. "Ting Ting will be fine. I will only be away for one month. Surely she'll be welcome in the home of one of her yimas for that time."

Bo Yima hurriedly reassured her sister. "Of course Ting Ting would be welcome to stay in our home. You know that."

Mei Yima now spoke up. "If you are set on doing this foolish thing, can you not take Ting Ting with you?"

"You know that wouldn't be possible. The officials would be suspicious that our intent was to stay in Canada if we asked permission for Ting Ting to travel

14

with me. I had a hard enough time yesterday getting a visa for myself."

So that's what Mama was up to yesterday, thought Ting. *No wonder she didn't care if my teeth fell out.*

Then, in a tone they had all come to recognize as meaning there would be no more discussion or argument, Mei Yima said, "Then it is settled. There is no changing your stubborn mind; that much is clear. Ting Ting will come live with me. Shan and I will be happy to provide for her while you are away, and young Junjie will be equally happy to have a playmate."

This was almost too much for Ting to take in. Trying to remain calm and keep a look of studious concentration on her face was growing more difficult by the minute. Mama was going to fly away to this far-off country that had already claimed Baba? A part of Ting wanted to stand up and scream "No!" But the stubborn part of her, the part that was stronger, won out. She continued to quietly copy the characters the teacher had assigned earlier that day.

Then her yima's declaration that Ting would stay with them started to sink in. Both her aunt and uncle, Mei and Shan, were kind and she loved them very much. She knew she would be well cared for if she was to be in their home. Her cousin Junjie was another story entirely. Each of the sisters had just one child, owing to the policies of the central government in Beijing. Ting's cousin Junjie was the only male child of their generation in the family, and he thought he was much more important than the others. He continually taunted and teased Ting, finding ways to best her at every turn. That Junjie! There was no way she could stand living under the same roof as him. It was bad enough being in the same class all day at school. This thought caused her almost more distress than the thought of her mama leaving her and going so far away.

Suddenly, Ting regretted her skilled eavesdropping of the discussion taking place at the Li family table.

· Chapter 3 ·

The next three months passed quickly. Someone was found to take care of the Li family's house while they were away. Mama, a doctor at the local hospital, had received special permission to be away from her work for a month. This wasn't hard to get, as everyone knew about Baba's special scholarship to study engineering in Canada, and knew what an honour this was. To deny Mama the time away would have been disrespectful, not only to the Li family, but more importantly to China itself.

School would occupy most of Ting's time while Mama was away. Classes started at eight in the morning, six days of the week, and ended at four-thirty every day except Saturday. Ting loved Saturdays! When the school doors opened to release the students at noon on Saturday, she felt the fresh air on her face and had a sense of freedom that eluded her within the school walls during the long, drawn-out week of monotonous memorization. Suddenly she had a whole afternoon and all the next day to fill with the things she most loved doing—reading books, painting, and playing with her friends. It also meant that, unless there was some special family event or an important holiday, she would have precious time away from her annoying cousin Junjie. Yes, Saturdays were usually the highlight of the week...but not today.

This was the day Mama was taking the train from Jinan, the city where they lived, to Beijing. She would stay in Beijing for two nights before flying to Vancouver, the city in Canada where Baba was a student. Ting had been given special permission to miss the morning's classes to go to the train station to say goodbye to her mama. Normally she would have been thrilled at the prospect of missing school...but not today.

Her stubbornness would not let Mama or her yimas see how much she was hurting on the inside, so she got up and tried to act as if it were an ordinary morning. The moment she stepped out of her room, she knew it would be impossible to pretend such a thing. There were her mama's two bags, packed and sitting ready to go, right in the path to the kitchen table. And when, out of habit, she glanced over at the small stand by the window to see how her fish were doing, she was met with an empty space. Her fish tank had been moved to Mei Yima's house yesterday, along with all the clothes and other things she would need over the course of the next four weeks. In spite of the fact they had not yet left, the house already had a feeling of emptiness about it.

"Hurry, Ting Ting. You must eat your breakfast quickly so we have time to get to the station before my train leaves." Mama was gesturing toward the table with hands that were holding several items—paperwork, money, keys. "Your yimas will be here any minute to drive us. Hurry!"

Eating was something Ting usually had no problem doing, but today she looked at her food and knew she could not touch it. Shoving it away when Mama placed it in front of her, she got up from the table and went to collect the few things she hadn't moved to her yima's yet, such as her toothbrush and pajamas. In another sign that this day was anything but ordinary, Mama ignored the fact that she wasn't eating and scurried on about her business. Normally a refusal to eat would have had Mama putting a hand on her forehead to check her temperature and asking her a thousand questions to make sure she wasn't getting sick.

Just then there was a knock on the door, followed by noisy greetings being exchanged among the sisters. Concerned looks were cast her way, but Ting pretended not to notice. She was determined not to show her sadness. There was another flurry of activity as they all fought over who should take which bag, followed by a quick check to make sure nothing had been left behind. As Ting watched the front door of their home being locked, she tried to think only of the time, a few short weeks from now, when it would once again be opened. If she could just keep thinking about that time, it might stop the sadness she felt growing inside her, threatening to burst out as tears.

When they arrived at the train station, with everyone a bit crumpled from being squeezed into the small car Mei Yima had borrowed, there was another argument over who would carry which bag. Ting thought this might be the way her yimas were dealing with their sadness over having their sister go so far away. Maybe bickering kept their sad thoughts from growing inside them. As they walked to the front entrance, she noticed Bo Yima reach up and quickly wipe her hand across her face, and Ting knew she had been right. Sadness surrounded them all, even if they pretended otherwise.

No sooner had they walked into the train station than Mama's train departure was being announced. Train departures always created a degree of chaos, and this one was made worse by the fact that Mama had two bags to get on the train. There was a surge of people toward the gate that allowed passengers through to the tracks. Without any warning Mama was caught up in the moving crowd and pulled out of Ting's reach. There was no chance for a goodbye hug or kiss. There wasn't even time for words to be spoken, words promising they would soon be together again, that Mama loved her, and that she would send Ting's greetings and love to Baba when she saw him.

One second she was there, and the next she was gone. And in that moment all of Ting's resolve to remain strong and courageous dissolved. She cried out in a wail that could be heard above all the noise of the surrounding crowd.

"Mama, don't leave me! Please, Mama, don't leave me!"

· Chapter 4 ·

The next week seemed like a month. Every day Ting would rush home from school, hoping to see a letter from Mama, or to hear her yima say there had been a phone call. Finally, on Friday, just when she thought she might explode from the suspense, Mei Yima met her at the door with a big smile on her face.

"Your mama has called all the way from Vancouver, Canada. She is with your baba and they're very happy to be together. They both send their love, and she said to be a good girl. I told her she did not have to worry, that you were bringing honour to your parents."

"Did she say anything else? Does she like Canada? Is Baba happy at his school?"

"I'm sorry, Ting Ting. Our call was very short. Phone calls from foreign countries are expensive, and the connection was poor. I could barely make out what your mama was saying. There wasn't time to say anything else. Besides, she will be home in no time at all, and then you can ask her all these things in person."

Part of Ting was happy because she now knew Mama was safe, but another part of her felt unsettled. There were so many questions she had, so many things she *needed* to know but that Baba might not have wanted to worry them with. Was he eating enough? Who knew what strange food they were serving in that faraway place! Was he succeeding at school? She worried that maybe he would not be able to keep up, since he spoke almost no English.

And was he warm enough? They had studied Canada at school last year, and she remembered it was a cold country with strange houses called igloos. Were her parents staying in an igloo? Were they safe? Their teacher last year had taught them about the fights between the native people and the early settlers and traders. Ting knew that had all happened a long time ago, but there might still be some hard feelings, much like many Chinese still harboured hard feelings toward the Japanese because of what they did during the war. Was it safe to encounter one of these natives, or might they still be angry enough to harm someone? There were so many things she wondered about, and now she might have to wait until Mama returned to find out the answers.

• • •

The second week went even slower than the first, if such a thing were possible. There were no phone calls or letters, the weather was cold and grey, and Junjie was even more annoying than usual. Mei Yima disciplined him when she caught him doing something wrong, but that was the problem. Junjie was sneaky and managed to escape his mama's watchful eye most of the time. Shan Yifu left most of the child-raising up to his wife and tended to be blind to all but the most glaring of Junjie's many faults.

For instance, on Monday morning Junjie had taken some hot chili powder out of the kitchen and sprinkled it into Ting's congee. Without looking at the contents of her bowl, which had assumed an unnatural shade of pale orange, Ting scooped up a big spoonful of the rice porridge and placed it in her mouth. She let out a yelp as she placed the ceramic spoon in her mouth, realizing too late that the congee was spicy hot. She quickly reached for her glass of water and managed to tip her yifu's cup of tea onto the morning newspaper he was trying to read. Shan Yifu scolded her for being clumsy, while Junjie looked on with a big grin on his face. Ting opened her mouth to explain, only to be cut off by Mei Yima, who came into the room telling them they needed to hurry or they would be late for school.

Never mind, Ting had thought. *I'll pay you back later, you weasel of a cousin.*

Things weren't much better at school than they were at home. Not only was Ting the smartest of all the cousins, but she was also the top student in her class at school. Teacher Chen would often hold her up as an example before the whole class. Junjie, however, was a very fast runner and good at all sports. He was the table tennis champion of their school, and last year he had won second place at the city-wide martial arts tournament. There were many award certificates decorating the walls of his home, and Junjie would make a point of explaining what each one was even though Ting had heard his stupid stories many times before. Respect for Yima and Yifu was all that kept her from taking each one of the worthless pieces of paper and ripping them up before Junjie's very eyes. That and the thought that all Junjie's sports awards were not going to help him gain entrance to the university. Ting's brain power was what was needed to secure one of those coveted spots.

And that was what made Monday afternoon's character writing class even worse than it might have been. Teacher Chen had warned the class that there would be a test that day, and the week before had given them a list of thirty characters to study. Ting had diligently practised her characters every spare moment she had, when she wasn't too worried about her mama to concentrate.

She used her favourite study method, which was to take out small sheets of paper and copy out five characters on each one. Then she would master one piece of paper at a time. It took only a few days until she knew all thirty characters, and in the meantime she didn't feel overwhelmed. It was Mama who had originally suggested this method, saying it had worked for her all the way through her courses at the university.

As Teacher Chen handed out blank pieces of writing paper to the students, Ting felt confident that she would once again get the top mark. The teacher spoke each character, walking up and down the rows of desks to observe his students' stroke order as they wrote, an important part of character writing. Ting easily reproduced the characters on her sheet. Just before Teacher Chen came up her aisle, Ting noticed a slight movement to her left but was too busy concentrating to look and see what had caused it. Just then Teacher Chen arrived at her desk, looked down, and picked something up from underneath it. Ting looked up as the teacher slowly unfolded a small scrap of paper, a concerned look on his face.

"Li Ting, is this your piece of paper?"

With a terrible feeling growing someplace deep in the pit of her stomach, Ting looked at the paper and recognized it as one of her study sheets. "But how ..." she started, only to be cut off by the teacher's stern voice.

"Li Ting, you will stay after the class is dismissed. Cheating is a very serious offence."

Ting could feel her face grow warm with humiliation. Never before had she been spoken to in this stern manner by her teacher. Never before had she been accused of cheating! There had to be some explanation for how that piece of paper had gotten under her desk. Could it have been stuck, unnoticed, on a piece of her clothing and fallen off as she sat down? Surely she would have noticed it sticking to her clothes, or her best friend, Yin, would have seen it and said something. No, it seemed highly unlikely that the paper had been on her when she sat down at her desk. Then how...The moment those two words popped into her head, so did a memory of that slight movement she had noticed right before Teacher Chen made his horrifying discovery.

The movement had come from her left, which was exactly where Junjie's desk sat.

· · ·

The rest of that school day passed like Junjie's pet turtle crawling across the bottom of its tank. It was one slow moment after another, coming ever closer to the time she would have to face Teacher Chen and his accusation. Respect was an important part of Chinese culture, taught to children from the time they took their first steps. Even two-year-olds, still walking around with a slit in the bottom of their pants because they were too little to use the toilet, knew they didn't dare sit down until the oldest person in the room had been seated ahead of them. Students knew from the moment they first entered the school that teachers must be obeyed and respected. Ting knew she couldn't argue with Teacher Chen about what he had found or question the conclusions he had drawn, even if he was mistaken. *But what do I do?* she thought. No matter how many times she played the scene over in her mind, she could not come up with a solution.

As it turned out, it was Junjie's own stupidity that gave him away. When the class was dismissed for the day, he turned to Ting and, with a look of triumph on his face, said in a voice loud enough for everyone to hear, "I knew you wouldn't be walking home with me, so I told Mama before I left this morning I was going over to Yong's to play after school." Still wearing that smirk Ting so despised, Junjie turned to exit the classroom.

"Wang Junjie, you will also stay," said Teacher Chen.

It was a simple statement spoken in a soft voice, but it carried with it an immense amount of power. Those six words instantly resulted in two things. They wiped the smirk off Junjie's face, and they put hope in Ting's heart. Now with the look of a cornered animal on his face, Junjie again showed his slowness of thought. As the teacher held up the crumpled piece of paper and asked Junjie if he knew what it was, Junjie said, "That's Ting's study note. She was using it at home. I saw her with it."

"You appear to know quite a few things, Wang Junjie. Not only do you seem to be aware of your cousin's study habits, habits I would hope you are going to adopt yourself after such close observation, but you also seem to be able to predict the future. Somehow you knew that Ting would be staying after class. Can you explain the source of this power to me, please?"

Junjie hung his head in shame, mumbling his apologies to both Teacher Chen and Ting. Teacher Chen then turned to Ting and said, "You may go home. I didn't really think you had cheated on the exam, Li Ting." Turning back to Junjie he said, "You will write a formal letter of apology to your parents for the shame you have brought on your family. You will also take Ting's place in the cleaning roster for the rest of the year."

Ting could not believe it! She hadn't uttered a word,

yet everything had managed to right itself. Teacher Chen did not think she had cheated. Junjie had finally been caught in one of his nasty pranks. And, almost best of all, she would not have to do the dreaded school cleaning for the rest of the year.

In China, all boys and girls cleaned their own classrooms. In this way, students assumed responsibility for their environment, knowing that it was they themselves who were going to clean up any messes. They were more careful because of this policy, but still, Ting hated it when it was her group's turn to take on cleaning duties. As she turned to leave the classroom that day, it was with a lighter heart than she'd had since Mama had left.

Chapter 5

Ting was so happy when she got out of bed a few mornings later. Mama would be coming home in just one more week. Two days ago a postcard had arrived in the mail for Ting. It had a picture of totem poles and said it was from a place called Stanley Park. Also— and this was what Ting was most excited about—it was June 1, Children's Day, and she and her friend Yin had been looking forward to it for days.

Yin and Ting had been best friends for as long as Ting could remember. They had been anticipating for days what kinds of candies they might receive on Children's Day. Not only would there be candy to eat, but they also knew there would be no home-work that day. Their class would be spending the day at Ting's favourite park—the one that had marble "slides" in front of the temple. Of course, they weren't really slides. They were the marble slabs on each side of the stairs leading up to the temple, slabs that had deep grooves worn into them from the countless children who had slid down them over the years.

The day ended up being just as tasty and just as much fun as Ting and Yin had hoped. That evening, feeling tired and happy, Ting was in the bathroom brushing her teeth with extra care—she had received both a stick candy *and* some hawthorn berry candy. She had just finished her teeth when she heard her yima and yifu talking in hushed tones at the kitchen table.

"I don't like this, Mei," said Shan Yifu.

"You know how the government is, Shan. They don't want to appear weak, but at the same time they want the world's approval. They will not do anything rash, I am certain."

"Still, with this disturbance going on in Beijing, I hope Li Shu doesn't have trouble there next week when she returns from Canada."

It was at that moment that Ting appeared in the hallway, pajamas on and teeth brushed. The conversation came to an abrupt halt, but Ting could see the worried expressions on Yima's and Yifu's faces. What did this mean? What was happening in Beijing? She desperately wanted to ask Yima, but she knew she was not meant to have heard the conversation. Once again Ting found herself sorry her listening skills were so good.

• • •

Over the next few days Ting noticed that the adults around her had serious looks on their faces and talked quietly among themselves. Even Teacher Chen was in a bad mood. The whole class trembled every time he spoke because he used such stern tones. During their daily exercise time out in the huge, open gravel area at the side of the school, there was none of their usual talk and laughter. The teacher who directed them barked at anyone who made a sound, resulting in a cloud of silence hanging over the students as they went through the familiar calisthenics. It made the boring routine of stretches, jumping jacks, and toe touches seem even worse than usual.

It was all very strange, and Ting knew it must have something to do with what she'd heard Yima and Yifu discussing the other night. She also knew that the "something" they were discussing involved the government, which meant it couldn't be openly discussed until everyone thought it was safe to do so. Nobody wanted to get on the wrong side of the central authorities in Beijing.

A few days before Mama was due to come home, Ting asked Yima if she could go play at Yin's for a little while before she did her schoolwork. Yima had a distracted look on her face and didn't appear to be listening. Just when Ting was about to repeat her question, Mei Yima said, "No, Ting Ting. I would like you to do your homework right now. There's something Yifu and I must discuss with you when he gets home. I would like your work finished before he arrives."

Disappointed, Ting opened her mouth to try to change Yima's mind but instantly closed it again when she saw the look on her face. She had never seen such a look before, one of fear and anger and confusion all swirling around together. *What does this mean?* Ting asked herself as she headed to her room to study.

It wasn't until two hours later that Shan Yifu finally

came in the door. He sighed as he sat down at the table. Mei Yima placed a cup of hot tea in front of him with one hand and patted him comfortingly on the shoulder with the other.

"The news is not good, Mei." He sighed again, then continued. "We need to speak with Ting. She needs to hear what has happened, even if she's too young to understand it all."

Ting scurried away from the door where she had been listening and back to her chair, grabbing her pen as she sat down. She was busy writing when Yima got to the bedroom door, and Ting pretended not to notice she was there.

"Ting Ting, Yifu and I would like for you to come into the kitchen. There are some serious matters we need to discuss."

Ting looked up at her yima, standing there wringing her hands, her cheeks all red and her usually neatly combed short hair sticking out. Even if Mei Yima had not said things were serious, one look at her would have given that fact away. When Ting entered the kitchen and saw the same look on Yifu's face, she suddenly felt so afraid she could barely breathe.

"What is it?" she said, her voice trembling. "Has something happened to Mama and Baba?"

Mei Yima reached out and enveloped Ting's hands in hers. "No, Ting Ting," she said, "your parents are both well. Yifu spoke with them on the phone this very afternoon."

At this news Ting's head jerked around to face her

yifu. "What did they say? Is Mama excited to return to China? Is Baba sad that she's going?"

"They are both fine, just as Yima told you. Baba has been eating better now that he has had Mama there, and Mama has managed to learn how to say a few words in English. She promises to teach them to you when she sees you again."

It was here that her yifu paused, looking as if he didn't know what to say next. Ting's patience finally ran out as she waited and waited for Shan Yifu to continue. "What, Yifu? What is it you need to tell me?" She hadn't meant to raise her voice, but her words were definitely delivered in a tone that normally would have resulted in a severe scolding. This time, however, no such reprimand was issued.

Yifu Shan cleared his throat and began telling Ting what had happened in Beijing over the past few days and weeks. Students had gathered at Tiananmen Square. They were protesting government policies and asking for more freedom for the people of China. More and more students gathered, until there were tens of thousands filling the square and surrounding streets of Beijing. The students had been peaceful, filled with hope that change could come to their country. Then, on June 4, tanks entered the streets and soldiers started shooting at the students. Hundreds of students had died, along with the dream of democracy for their country.

"I am sorry you have to hear about such awful things, but there is a reason I must tell you about them.

The government is punishing some of the students, and not just the students who were involved at Tiananmen Square. There is talk that some Chinese students studying in foreign countries supported the students here. Because some were involved, all will be suspected."

Shan Yifu paused again as Ting looked at him in rising horror. "Ting Ting, it would be dangerous for your baba to return to China right now, and we aren't sure if your mama should come home without him."

• Chapter 6 •

When Shan Yifu was finished talking, his shoulders slumped and his head dropped down so his eyes were focused on the floor. It was as if the weight of what he had just said was too much to bear. Not even when she did not fully understand what he was telling her had Ting interrupted with a question. It wasn't that she didn't *want* to ask questions. She had a hundred questions scurrying around inside her head, more questions than she had ever had in her life. But she knew that if she opened her mouth, more than just questions would come pouring out. Her deep fear for her parents, her longing to see Mama and Baba again, her loneliness, her hatred for her cousin Junjie—all of it would come flooding out in sobs she would not be able to stop, sobs that would say more than mere words ever could. So she sat there as still as the stone statues that dotted nearby Thousand Buddha Mountain, Yima Mei's hands still wrapped around her own smaller ones.

Ting looked over to the corner where her fish tank was set up, then into the kitchen where her yima had vegetables chopped and ready to throw into the wok for their dinner, then out onto the street where there was a Uighur cart selling *yang rou chuan*, the Chinese lamb kebabs she loved so much. All these scenes were so familiar to her. They were things she had seen her whole life, some of the many ordinary parts that fit together to make the life she knew and loved here in this neighbourhood, in this city, and, she thought with a sense of stubborn pride, in this country—even if some things the government was doing right now were bad. It was all so familiar, yet suddenly everything had changed.

It was with this thought that Ting quietly got up and started walking toward her room at the end of the hall. I can do this. *I can make it to my room without disgracing myself in front of Yima and Yifu.*

She was not sure if she could make it to her room before sobs overtook her, but just then she noticed Junjie staring at her from the doorway to his bedroom. That gave her the added bit of resolve she needed as she stiffened her back and kept moving forward.

It wasn't until the door was safely shut behind her that Ting allowed herself to cry. The tears started slowly at first, one after the other, rolling down her cheeks in a steady stream. That stream soon became a river as Ting cried harder and harder, sobs racking her skinny frame. What had Yifu meant when he'd said it might not be safe for Mama to come home? Surely the soldiers who fired the guns would not want to hurt her mama. Mama was a kind, good-hearted woman. She worked to make people better, not hurt them. Why would anyone want to hurt her? Mama had nothing to do with this place of trouble called Tiananmen Square!

An hour later, when her yima opened the door, she discovered Ting asleep on the floor, cuddled up with the blanket she had slept with since she was a tiny baby. Now in tatters, and a different colour than it had started out, it still had the power to comfort Ting when she was sad. Ting stirred slightly as Mei Yima scooped her into her arms and gently laid her on the bed, slipping off her shoes and pants, then sliding her under the covers. She felt a soft kiss on her forehead, then heard Yima speaking quietly to Yifu.

"It's best for her to sleep. Tomorrow she will feel rested and the shock of the news will be past. We can only hope that things will be better then."

• • •

When Ting woke up in the morning her eyes felt peculiar, and her first thought was that Junjie must have sneaked in during the night and tried to glue her eyelids together. Then, when she looked down and saw she was still wearing her school uniform shirt rather than her pajamas, the memories of yesterday came flooding back, filling her with despair. Shan Yifu had said they did not know *if* Mama would be able to return. He had not said they did not know *when* Mama would return.

Whatever could this mean? How could Mama not return to China? China was her home. Ting was here waiting for her. Mama had her important job at the hospital. They had their little house around the corner waiting for them to return. Every day on her way home from school, Ting would look at their little house and think about how lonely it seemed. She tried to imagine how it had been before Mama left, with good smells coming from the open windows and clothes hanging to dry from the pole sticking out of the back wall. It was nicer to think of it that way than how it was now—dark and empty, lonely and lifeless.

Ting was very slow in getting ready for school that morning. She was so slow that by the time she walked into the kitchen for breakfast she saw that Junjie had already left for school. Mei Yima came over to the table with a bowl of salty soft-tofu soup for Ting, a smile firmly fixed on her face.

"I'm sorry, Yima. I don't think I have time to eat this. I'm going to be late for school."

"It's okay, Ting Ting. Today you may stay home from school. I have sent a note with Junjie explaining to the teacher that you are unwell."

Ting looked at her yima in surprise. Mei Yima never lied!

As if reading her mind, Mei Yima continued, "There are other kinds of sickness than fevers and stomach complaints. A broken heart needs as much care as a cold. Today Bo Yima and I are going to do our best to help your heart heal."

· Chapter 7 ·

What followed would have been one of the most wonderful days of Ting's life, if only she had not had the horrible news about Mama and Baba to spoil it. The day was clear and bright, promising the first scorching hot weather of the year. Before the sun heated up everything around them, the yimas decided, they would climb Thousand Buddha Mountain.

The base of Thousand Buddha Mountain was only a five-minute walk from Mei Yima's home. It wasn't really a mountain at all, but to have called it a mere hill would have been insulting to the statues of Buddha scattered all over it. There weren't really a thousand of them, but there *were* hundreds. There had been even more, but many had been smashed by the Red Guards during the Cultural Revolution. That dark time in China had ended over a decade ago, before Ting had even been born. Buddha was no longer considered an enemy of the people, and Thousand Buddha Mountain had once again become a favourite place for the residents to get some fresh air and exercise. No matter how many times she climbed the mountain, Ting never grew tired of the view of her city.

By the time they arrived at the top, Ting's thoughts of Mama had been replaced by thoughts of food. Ting loved to eat, and her family often teased her by asking if she had a secret place she was storing all that she ate, for it always seemed more than one skinny girl could manage. The climb left her ravenous, and the smells coming from the various vendors' carts made her stomach growl. Bo Yima looked at Ting when she heard the growls and laughed. "We'd better feed you before those loud noises coming from your stomach wake up the sleeping Buddha at the top of the hill."

Ting smiled up at Bo Yima and said, "I wouldn't want to get in trouble for disturbing the Buddha."

Bo Yima walked over to the cart selling thin strips of pork layered one on top of the other, a wooden stick holding them all together. When she handed Ting the skewer of meat, sizzling hot and smelling wonderful, Ting suddenly remembered that she hadn't eaten any supper the night before. No wonder she was so hungry! Then she remembered *why* she hadn't eaten supper, and the smile disappeared from her face.

The earlier hints of the first heat wave of the summer proved true, and by the time the yimas and Ting finished their snacks and hiked down to the bottom of the hill, they were tired and sweaty.

"Can we go cool off at the park? Please?" Ting looked up at her yimas, hoping they were as hot as she was.

"Yes, but first I think we need to buy a treat from the cold cart over by the park entrance," said Bo Yima.

Ting was surprised by this suggestion. Although

40

their families were not poor, they were also not rich. Money had to be watched closely, and there had already been the treat at the top of the mountain. "Are you sure, Bo Yima?"

"Yes, she is sure," said Mei Yima.

That certainly settled it, then, as no one would dare argue with Mei Yima! The three of them walked over to the cart and looked at the offerings. Bo Yima loved chocolate, so it was no surprise when she pointed to the ice cream bar. Mei Yima took a little longer to decide, but in the end picked the corn-flavoured frozen treat, the one in the yellow and green wrapper with a picture of a corncob on the front. Ting looked longingly at all the treats in the small freezer, but in the end she chose what she always did—the hawthorn berry bar. "*Xie xie*," she said, remembering to thank the man as he handed her the ice-cold treat.

As they walked toward the park entrance gate in silence, concentrating on eating their bars before they melted in the hot sun, Ting thought again about Mama. Part of her wanted to ask Mei Yima what Shan Yifu had meant when he said that horrible word *if*. Had he meant Mama might not *ever* be coming back to China—and to Ting? Just as she got up the courage to open her mouth and ask, Bo Yima grabbed her hand and pulled her along. "Come on, Ting Ting! I'm hot and need to cool my feet."

In addition to Thousand Buddha Mountain, Jinan was famous for two other reasons. The first was its proximity to Taishan, one of China's five great mountains and a World Heritage Site. The second was the city's numerous natural wells that provided the people with free, clean, good-tasting water. It was a common sight to see people hurrying down the street with their empty jugs, or lumbering back with their overflowing containers, water slopping over the sides as they went along. Several parks in the city had made use of the natural springs to fill small pools with water, providing a place for young and old alike to cool off on a hot day.

Chomping down the last bites of her treat, Ting hurried along beside her yimas. When they got to the pool—a big concrete structure shaped like a horseshoe—there was a race to see who could get her sandals off fastest and be first in the water. Surprisingly, it was Bo Yima who made the first big splash! Seeing her yimas giggle like young schoolgirls made Ting giggle as well, in spite of the sorrow and uncertainty deep inside her. The three of them chased and splashed each other until they were soaked to the bone. It felt good to be cool again, and it felt good to laugh.

Later, as they walked into their own neighbourhood again, Ting's yimas had one more surprise for her. Of all the foods in the world Ting could think of, there was nothing she liked better than the *yang rou chuan* sold from the cart at the end of their street. The vendor was Uighur. This ethnic group lived in the northwest corner of China, but a small number of them had moved throughout the country, setting up the popular stands wherever they went. A long trough would be filled on the bottom with red-hot charcoal. Sitting on top of the trough, in little slots that allowed them to be turned to cook on all sides, were the bamboo skewers filled with chunks of fresh lamb.

One man ran the stand, taking money and handing out the skewers. Another man, or in an especially busy time, such as a festival, maybe two or even three more men, would be busy constantly rotating the skewers so the meat was done to perfection. As they turned the meat, they would pick up a shaker with a mysterious powder in it and sprinkle this over the top, sending up an irresistible smell.

The yimas bought three skewers and handed one to Ting. Taking a bite, Ting thought there couldn't ever be anything better. When she was little, she'd thought the man with the can was shaking a magic powder over the meat, giving it its special flavour. Now that she was older she knew, of course, that there was nothing magic in the can. But she did often wonder just what *was* in that can. If it wasn't magic, it had to be something very close!

With her stomach feeling full and her heart feeling content, at least for the moment, the three of them headed back, hand in hand, to Mei Yima's. Though she didn't know it, her aunts' actions that day had forever embedded in Ting's mind the sights, sounds, and smells of Jinan, the city of her birth. In later years when Ting thought longingly of her childhood, the pictures that most frequently came to mind were snapshots of that wonderful, special day with her yimas.

· Chapter 8 ·

The next two months moved by at a pace even slower than Teacher Chen's Chinese history class. Ting would not have thought that possible before the day in June when the bad things in Beijing had happened. Ting respected Teacher Chen, but that did not mean she had to like his history class. All they ever talked about were dynasties. Under which dynasty did this event happen? During which dynasty did that person rule? Through what years did this dynasty extend? Dynasty this and dynasty that, until Ting thought her head might explode. It was all so long ago, and who cared about a bunch of dead people anyway? This was modern China and there were no more dynasties, which Ting decided was a good thing if for no other reason than it would keep more from being added to the tedious list schoolchildren had to memorize.

At last, summer vacation arrived. The month-long holiday from school was usually something Ting looked forward to. It was a time when she was free from the confines of the school walls for weeks on end, a time when she and Mama and Baba would do something special together. One year they took the train to Qingdao, a city by the sea. Ting got to play all day on the beach, building sandcastles and swimming in the warm water. Another year they went to Beijing and saw the Temple of Heaven and the Forbidden City. Ting hadn't liked that trip as much as the one to the sea, probably because there was too much talk about dynasties when she was in Beijing, and in Qingdao the conversation was mostly about what kind of seafood they would eat for dinner that night.

But this year, with all the uncertainty, Ting had nothing special to look forward to. Yin and her family had gone to Shanghai to visit relatives. They had invited Ting to go with them, and the girls had immediately started making plans. The journey to Shanghai was very long, so long they would get to sleep on the train! Pulling out the little bed and closing her eyes while the train kept moving through the dark night, then waking in the morning in a faraway city—it all sounded so exciting.

Then, a few days before she was supposed to go, she overheard Shan Yifu say, "Mei, we cannot let Ting take this trip with Yin's family. You know that, don't you?"

"But surely, Shan, it will be okay for her to be gone for just the week? Nothing will be happening this week. It's too soon."

It was at this point that Junjie came crashing into her bedroom door, a soccer ball at his feet. "Ouch," exclaimed Ting, holding the side of her face the door had slammed into.

"What are you doing standing there, anyway? Isn't your name supposed to mean 'graceful'? I think your parents made a big mistake when they named you. You can't even stand in one spot without doing something clumsy."

"Junjie!" Shan Yifu shouted from the kitchen. "Come here *now*."

The surprised look on Junjie's face at hearing his father speak in such a stern tone was almost worth the bruise Ting would surely have on her cheek the next morning. For once he had been caught in his meanness. Ting hoped Shan Yifu would deal with him harshly.

Sometime later there was a knock on her door. Ting said, "Come in," expecting to see her yima come in to talk to her. Instead it was Junjie. He had an odd look on his face, one Ting had never seen before.

"Ting Ting, I'm sorry I hurt you. And I'm sorry I said those mean things about your name to you. Please forgive me."

Ting was so shocked to hear those words come out of her cousin's mouth that she found herself saying, "I forgive you, Junjie." She hadn't wanted to say it, and she wasn't even sure she meant it, but it was too late. She couldn't take the words back now. When she saw genuine relief on her cousin's face, she found herself smiling at him. It was a small smile, but a smile all the same.

"Would you like to play a game of *weiqi?*"

Ting tried to hide her surprise at Junjie's request. She shrugged her shoulders as if it didn't really matter

46

to her either way and nonchalantly said, "I guess so, if you do."

"Sure. You always win, but who knows, maybe tonight I'll get lucky."

"That is what is wrong with you, Junjie. You don't understand that winning the game has nothing to do with luck. It is a game that involves thinking."

Ting's sharp words broke the spell that had somehow overtaken her cousin, and he retorted in a way that sounded more like his usual self. "All that thinking you do must be the reason your head is lopsided."

At this they both smiled, then headed to the corner to get the game from its storage place under the chair. And, as Ting had predicted, she soundly beat her cousin.

The next day, however, Ting's aunt and uncle told her what she already knew: there would be no trip to Shanghai with Yin. There would be no adventure sleeping on the train. There would be no ferry ride on the Huangpu River. What they did not tell Ting, but what she most wanted to know, was *why*. Why couldn't she go with Yin?

Yin's parents were very responsible people. They would not let anything bad happen to her. They were also very wealthy and had insisted on paying for Ting's trip, saying it was doing them a favour because it would help keep Yin out of trouble. So money could not be the reason she had to stay home. And what had Mei Yima meant when she said, "Nothing will be happening this week. It is too soon"?

So here she was with nothing to do, and that nothingness gave Ting far too much time to worry about her circumstances. She wanted her life to go back to the way it had been before Mama left for Canada, back even to the way it had been before Baba had been honoured with the scholarship. Ting wished she had never heard of that place called Canada.

Just when she thought her head might explode from so much worry, something unexpected happened. Mei Yima told her that she and Bo Yima would be taking her to the village where Yeye lived. Ting was surprised by this news, not because she was going to see her yeye, but rather because it was her mama's sisters who were taking her. Yeye was Baba's father and had no connection with Bo Yima and Mei Yima. It seemed very strange that they should be making this journey with her. Since this was not something Ting had learned about through her eavesdropping endeavours, she realized she was free to voice her confusion. "Why are you and Bo Yima taking me to see Yeye, Mei Yima? You don't even know him." Suddenly Ting had a horrid thought. "Is Yeye sick?"

"No, Ting Ting, Yeye is well. I spoke with him last night and his voice was very strong. Bo Yima and I just felt it was time for you to pay a visit to him. You are lonely and he is lonely. You can give each other comfort."

Ting thought about this for a minute, still not fully convinced her yima was telling her everything, but said, "Thank you, Mei Yima. I would very much like to see my yeye."

It was true. Ting loved going to visit Yeye. He had been alone for many years. His wife, Ting's nainai, had died before Ting was born. But Yeye was not really alone. He had chickens that ran around his yard—and through his house if Ting forgot to close the door. He also had three songbirds, each one a different colour. The largest and loudest was a brilliant blue, the next in size was red with splotches of black on its wings, and the littlest one was a yellow every bit as bright as the sun. The birds were kept in separate cages that Yeye had made himself.

Sometimes when Ting was visiting, she and Yeye would take one of the cages to the nearby park, where Yeye would hang it on the branch of a tree. Then he would sit down at one of the benches where other elderly men had congregated, sometimes joining in one of the never-ending games of *weiqi*, and other times just gossiping with the men. Ting was free to go exploring as long as she didn't wander too far from Yeye. She always felt such freedom when she was on her own in the small forest in the park.

Yes, she thought, *I would very much like to see Yeye.*

· Chapter 9 ·

The train journey to Yeye's took only half an hour. Ting wished it were longer, not because she wasn't eager to see her yeye, but simply because she loved riding the train. Once they were out of the city she could see the fields stretching in all directions. Dotting the fields, like game pieces set up on a board, were workers bent over tending their crops. Ting was glad she didn't have to work in the fields all day. *It must be very hard work*, she thought.

When they arrived at Yeye's, she gave him a big hug, then introduced her yimas. Yeye gave them each one of his big, toothless smiles, then invited them in for tea. It was impossible not to be happy around Yeye, and she could see by the smiles on her yimas' faces that they must feel the same way.

Ting knew there would be no trip to the park with Yeye that day. The yimas had explained that they must be back to the city before it got dark, so they could stay to visit for only a short while. Still, Ting was *so* happy to be there. The chickens followed and pecked at her legs as she walked to the front door, but she outsmarted them and closed the door quickly behind her so they couldn't come in, which had clearly been their intent.

When they sat around the table to drink their tea, Yeye held a stick of candy-coated hawthorn berries in front of Ting. Her eyes lit up when she saw it. The berries were covered in a hard red candy, as bright as a shiny ripe apple. Inside were the tart hawthorn berries. When you bit into one of these treats, the tang of the berry mixed with the sweetness of the candy coating in a perfect burst of flavour.

"*Xie xie!*" Ting exclaimed, taking the candy from Yeye's outstretched hand.

As Ting savoured her candy, she listened to the grown-ups talking around her. The conversation flitted from one topic to another. The weather, the crops this year, the latest reports out of Beijing, all things Ting found dull. When she had finished her hawthorn candy, Yeye asked her if she could please go out and feed the chickens, and if she could then go pick a bowl of strawberries from the little patch at the back of his house.

Ting jumped up and was out the door in a flash! She didn't care about feeding the chickens. It was a task she found annoying. Chickens were such stupid birds, pecking at her and one another, scurrying about to try to eat the scraps of food all at once, and in the process squawking so loudly they made Ting's ears ring. But strawberries! Ting had not tasted a strawberry since last year when she was visiting Yeye. They weren't often found in the shops in Jinan, and even when Mama did come upon them at the market she refused to buy them, saying they were inferior to what she could get next time they visited Yeye. The thought of a whole bowl of fresh strawberries made Ting's mouth water.

By the time Ting returned with her bowl overflowing with berries, and telltale red streaks around her mouth indicating that some berries had never made it to the bowl, the grown-ups had finished their tea. Ting noticed they didn't have big smiles on their faces anymore. She hoped they were all getting along. She loved her yimas and Yeye very much and wanted them all to like each other. It would be unthinkable to have the special people in her life, the people she cared most about, not care for each other.

As they all sat sharing the strawberries Ting had picked, she was relieved to see smiles on everyone's faces again. They laughed over her messy face, and Yeye teased her, saying she might turn completely red if she ate even one more berry. All too soon she heard the words she had been dreading.

"Ting Ting, it's time for us to catch our train back to Jinan. You need to say goodbye to Yeye." It was Mei Yima talking, and that meant there was no use arguing about having to go. When Mei Yima made up her mind, there was no changing it. As they got up from the table, Yeye spoke.

"Ting Ting, I have something I would like for you to take with you." Walking over to the old chest that Ting had searched through many times before, Yeye opened it and retrieved an old brown album, its cover torn and several pages loose and hanging out the side. Ting knew right away what it was—the family photo album! Ting had spent hours looking through the old snapshots of Baba's family, imagining what each person was like at the time the picture was taken. Many people she did not know—they had died long before Ting's baby picture had made its entrance into the cherished album. But Yeye had told her their stories, so she felt as though she knew them all well.

Ting gasped as Yeye handed her the album, and she saw that he had tears in his eyes. He couldn't mean to give her this! "No, Yeye! I cannot accept this. It is your treasured family album. You need to have it with you to keep you company when you get lonely. I can look at it when I come to visit you."

A tear rolled down Yeye's cheek as he said, "No, Ting Ting, it is time for you to be the keeper of this book. You know its stories. They are in your head and in your heart. The book must stay with you now."

Knowing she could not say no, Ting reached out and took the album Yeye was holding out to her. Then, suddenly, he reached down and wrapped her in his arms, giving her a hug bigger than any he had ever given her before. She looked up into his eyes and said, "I promise to take good care of the album, Yeye. I will not forget the stories."

"Okay, Ting Ting, it's time for us to say goodbye." Ting looked over at Bo Yima and was surprised to see she, too, had tears in her eyes. Before she could stop to wonder why, Mei Yima was shooing her out the door, muttering something about being late and needing to get back to Jinan in time to stop at the vegetable market before that worthless vegetable seller ran out of fresh spring onions.

"Bye, Yeye! I will see you soon," Ting called out as the yimas hurried her along the narrow street. As she turned to wave goodbye to Yeye one last time, she noticed him brush his face with his arm, then slowly turn and walk back into his house.

• • •

Two days after the visit to Yeye's, Ting finally got answers to all those questions that had been building up inside of her. Mei Yima invited her into the kitchen and sat her down at the table, where Bo Yima was already seated. Immediately, Ting knew something horrible was coming.

"Ting Ting, we need to have a serious discussion. Two weeks ago your mama phoned me and said they had made up their minds."

Ting was hurt. She knew nothing of this phone call. Why hadn't Mei Yima told her that Mama had called? She knew how worried Ting was about her and how much she missed her.

Mei Yima could see the unasked question on Ting's face. "We had serious business to discuss in that phone call, Ting Ting. One never knows how long the phone connection will last, and we couldn't afford to take the chance that we would get cut off before everything was settled. If it had been a normal call, I would have let you speak with Mama; you must believe that."

At this point Bo Yima got up to get the teapot. Mei Yima waited until fresh cups of tea had been poured, then continued. "Your parents see no other choice than to remain in Canada. It is a good country, one filled with many people who have come from other lands. Your paperwork to leave China and join them has come through much faster than we had expected. You will be able to leave the day after tomorrow, and in the meantime we have many important things to do."

Mei Yima stopped talking. The room was filled with a sad silence, one that said nothing, but at the same time everything. Ting's first thought was *No! No, I cannot leave my home here in China and go to this faraway place.* However, another thought immediately followed. *But I have no choice. It is where Mama and Baba are, and they aren't coming back to China.*

Without saying a word, Ting stood up and slowly walked to her room.

·Chapter 10·

When Ting woke up the next morning, she thought of a thousand things she wanted to do on this, her last day in China. Tomorrow she would fly across the ocean to a new country and a new life. *Will I ever return to China, to my home?* she wondered. She thought of all the places she loved in Jinan—the parks, the pools filled with clean, cool water, Thousand Buddha Mountain, the street vendors selling their delicious food, the little house she had grown up in with Mama and Baba, and now that she knew she might never return, even her school.

Worse than the thought of leaving behind these familiar places was the thought of saying goodbye to the people she loved. Now she understood why Yeye had given her the family photo album, and why her yimas had taken her out on that day of adventure. She also understood why she hadn't been able to go with Yin and her family to Shanghai.

Yin! thought Ting with a sudden pang. Yin was in Shanghai and wouldn't return until next week. Ting would not have a chance to say goodbye to her! With this thought she burst into tears and collapsed across her bed, which is where Mei Yima found her an hour later, tears still running down her face as she clutched her blanket.

"Shh, Ting Ting," she said gently, taking Ting in her arms and holding her tightly.

"I...I..." Ting tried to get the words out but just couldn't. Mei Yima continued to hold her until she was finally able to talk. "I won't be able to say goodbye to Yin! I'll be gone before they get back to Jinan!" Sobs began anew as she spoke.

"I have thought of this, and so I bought you this present."

Ting looked up as Mei Yima pulled a package out from her pocket. It was wrapped in a beautiful red cloth embroidered with flowers and tied with a dark green silk ribbon. Slowly she reached out and took the package Mei Yima held in her hands. Carefully untying the ribbon and setting it and the beautiful cloth to one side to admire later, she pulled out a small box.

"It is writing paper. This way, as soon as you get to Canada you can write a letter to Yin to let her know you're well, and you can tell her what your new home is like. I have purchased a box for Yin as well, so she can write back and tell you about everything that is happening here. This way you will be able to remain friends, even if an ocean separates you."

"*Xie xie*," Ting said as she gave her yima another hug.

"Now get dressed. We have an important duty to see to."

An hour later Bo Yima joined them and they made

their way to the cemetery. Here were the urns holding the remains of Ting's grandparents—the parents of Mama and the yimas. Located partway up a large hill, the place of burial was surrounded by a tall fence. At the entrance was a small booth with an official sitting inside. Mei Yima handed the man a slip of paper with some numbers on it, and after checking through his stack of books he gave the yimas directions.

Even though they had been here many times, they needed directions because there were so many identical buildings at the cemetery, and each building had many rooms. Each of those rooms was filled with small compartments, and behind the glass door to each of these compartments was an urn, a picture of the deceased person, and a few mementoes from that person's life.

The yimas argued briefly over which way to turn, and at one point they had to backtrack and go a different direction, but finally they found the building they were looking for. Before they entered, Mei Yima explained to Ting the significance of her laolao's and laoye's remains resting in this particular building. Ting listened politely, even though she had heard about it before from Mama.

"This is the special place reserved for heroes of our country. Your laolao and laoye both fought against the Japanese when they invaded China."

"Laolao too?" Ting asked in surprise. This was a new piece of information, one Mama had neglected to tell her.

"Yes, Ting Ting. Things were so desperate at that time that even the women were called on to fight. Your laolao was very brave, as was your laoye. Only those who have shown great courage can rest here. It is a great honour to our family to have them here."

Ting watched as her yimas carefully removed each picture and the few small items behind the glass doors. Next they headed outside to a large circular structure in the centre of the grounds. The metal structure was divided into many sections, each large enough to hold the items that had been behind the glass doors inside the building. Mei Yima placed Laolao's in one compartment, while Bo Yima placed Laoye's in another. They reached into the bags they had brought with them from home and pulled out melons, mangoes, and apples. These were placed in front of the pictures. Next Bo Yima produced a bottle of wine from deep inside her bag, along with some small cups. She poured a small amount of wine into each cup and set them down at the base of the structure. Then she turned to Ting.

"It is time for us to pay our respects to our mama and baba—your laolao and laoye." She turned to face Laolao's picture and said, "Mama, I hope you are resting peacefully. We have brought Ting Ting with us to say her goodbyes to you. Tomorrow she'll travel to a new country and face many new adventures. We will make sure she never forgets you and your courage." Then Bo Yima bowed and looked over at Mei Yima.

Stepping in front of the compartment with Laoye's

picture, Mei Yima said in a clear, strong voice, "Baba, we all miss you very much, and after tomorrow we will all miss Ting very much. We promise to help her remember the country of her birth, and her ancestors who went before her." Mei Yima bowed, just as Bo Yima had done.

The three of them stood there silently for several minutes, and then her yimas took the little cups of wine and poured them on the ground in front of the sections holding the symbolic fruit, pictures, and trinkets. Everything was then gathered up, including the fruit, and they headed back to the heroes' building to replace the items they had taken. They walked back down the hill in silence. At the bottom, Mei Yima said, "Let's go over to the little park and have a rest."

When they sat down, Bo Yima reached into the pack, producing the fruits that had been used for the ceremony. Then she pulled out a knife and began to cut them into small pieces, handing some to Ting as she did so. The three of them sat there, eating the fruit and laughing and pointing at each other as the juice ran down their faces. It felt good to laugh after so much seriousness.

Then Mei Yima looked at Ting, and in her voice that indicated she was the eldest and therefore commanded respect, she said, "Ting Ting, you have just paid respect to your grandparents. They both showed great courage at a time when it was needed. You are their granddaughter, and I know you carry the same courage within you. It will be there for you when you need it."

• Chapter 11 •

After tossing and turning most of the night, Ting woke up the next morning with a sick feeling in her stomach. She had no time to think about her fears, though, because Mei Yima hurried her from the moment she got out of bed.

"Hurry, Ting Ting, get dressed quickly."

"Hurry, Ting Ting, eat your breakfast. We must go soon."

"Ting Ting, get your toothbrush and blanket in your bag right now. It's time to go."

In this way Mei Yima wisely managed to get her bundled and into the borrowed car before Ting had time to even think, much less be sad. Bo Yima would not be going to the airport. There wasn't room in the car for Ting, Shan Yifu, Mei Yima, Junjie, the two large suitcases Ting was taking with her, and Bo Yima's family, so they had said their goodbyes the day before.

If it had just been Ting's things, one suitcase would have been enough, but there were also things that belonged to her parents, important things that needed to be sent with her. Even though it was much more expensive, it had been decided that the best way to get Ting to Beijing, where she would later in the day board the flight taking her to Canada, was to send her from Jinan to Beijing on a small plane. An official from the airline would see to it that she got safely on the overseas flight.

When they got to the airport, Mei Yima was back in hurry-up mode.

"Quickly, Ting Ting, we need to walk this way."

"Junjie, keep up, we need to go faster."

"Shan, be careful with that bag. It has breakable things in it!"

By the time they got to the gate where Ting's plane was scheduled to depart, Mei Yima was out of breath from having barked out so many instructions. Shan Yifu's face was red from the strain of having lugged two huge bags through the airport, and Junjie had an odd look on his face, one Ting had never seen before. Ting watched as Mei Yima went up to the airline official by the gate to ask her something. Another official was called over, and after several more minutes of discussion, Mei Yima joined them again, a pleased look on her face. "The airline people have agreed that when it's time for you to board, we can accompany you to the stairs leading up into the plane."

No sooner had Yima said those words than an announcement was made over the loudspeaker saying that all passengers flying to Beijing on Air China flight number 314 were now to board the plane. Ting looked at Yima and Yifu with a panicked expression on her face.

Without saying a word, Mei Yima grabbed Ting's hand and quickly led her through the door and out onto the tarmac, Shan Yifu and Junjie following closely behind. It was at this point that Mei Yima ran out of avoidance tactics to keep Ting's mind off her upcoming journey. The time had come to say good-bye. They stood there, tearfully hugging and promising they would see each other soon, although none of them knew if this was actually true. The other passengers streamed by, avoiding eye contact as they made their way to the plane. After the last passenger had gone up the stairs, the flight attendant looked down at them and indicated Ting also needed to make her way up the steps.

Giving Mei Yima one last hug, Ting turned and slowly walked toward the plane. Just before she got to the stairs she felt someone tug her sleeve. Turning around, she was surprised to see it was Junjie. He still had that very strange look on his face. Without saying a word, he reached out and placed something in Ting's pocket. Then he turned and ran back to Yima and Yifu.

As Ting climbed the stairs she reached into her pocket and pulled out a small item wrapped in tissue paper. She gasped when she saw what it was: Junjie's most prized possession, a small, perfectly shaped jade panda. When she reached the top of the stairs, Ting turned and waved goodbye to him—and to the only home she had ever known. Then, tears streaming down her cheeks, she turned and made her way into the plane.

· Chapter 12 ·

Ting felt someone gently tapping her on the arm.

"Li Ting, we are almost to Vancouver. You need to wake up."

Ting popped her eyes open, looking around in confusion. Her head felt thick and her eyes felt as if they had bits of glass ground into them. Then, suddenly, she remembered. She was on an airplane on her way to see Mama and Baba, on her way to a new country. She looked up at the flight attendant and attempted to smile. The lady had been so kind to her during the long trip over the Pacific Ocean. She had brought her extra packets of cookies and some coloured pencils and a book to draw in. When she noticed Ting yawning and rubbing her eyes, she had brought her a blanket and miniature pillow. She had even helped Ting get her own special blanket out of Mei Yima's cloth bag tucked under the seat in front of her.

"Let me help you get your seat belt on. We'll be landing soon. The pilot says the weather in Vancouver today is very good—nothing but blue sky. You are lucky. It rains there often, but today you will be able to see the city *and* the mountains."

After the flight attendant walked away, Ting looked out the window. She had been lucky about that, too. When she got on the big plane in Beijing, she found herself seated between two men, both wearing suits and looking very serious. When the man next to the window overheard Ting talking to the flight attendant and realized this was her first time flying over the ocean, he offered to switch places with her.

"I have to work on a business proposal, so I won't have time to enjoy the view. Besides, I've done this trip many times before."

At first Ting was excited to be able to look out the window and see the ocean beneath her. When they took off from the airport in Beijing, she could look down at all the buildings and houses, just as she had when she'd left Jinan. But in no time at all they went through some clouds, and then all she could see was fluffy white underneath her. That soon became dull, so she turned her head away from the window and sighed. If it hadn't been for the kind lady, Ting was sure she would have died of boredom. Not only was it boring, but the man who had traded seats with her smelled bad, like the outer leaves of the cabbage Mama would chop up and cook in their wok. She had finally buried her face in her blanket in an attempt to block out the stench, and that was when she had fallen asleep.

Now that the flight was almost over, she found her stomach suddenly felt nervous, much like when Teacher Chen would call her up to the front of the class to speak. How would she find her parents when they got to the airport? Would anyone even be able to understand her if she needed to ask for help? She knew people spoke English in Canada, not Chinese. So far the only English words Ting knew were *hello*, *goodbye*, and *thank you*. None of those were going to help her if she got lost. Just when she thought she might start crying, the flight attendant came back and told her that when they landed, an escort would help her through customs and on to the arrival area where her parents would be waiting. Ting relaxed, stopped clutching her blanket, and turned to take in her first view of the land across the sea. The first things she noticed, probably because they were too big not to notice, were the mountains, standing tall like soldiers guarding the city.

The minute the plane came to a stop, the people around her jumped up and started opening the overhead bins, trying to be the first to get their bags. *How silly*, thought Ting. *We are all trapped here until the door is opened. Hurrying to get your bag is not going to get you off the plane any faster.* Eventually the door did open, and the passengers quickly started filing past.

Ting had been told to wait until everyone had left, and then the escort would be there to help her. She was glad she was able to wait. As cramped as her legs felt, and as much as she wanted to see her parents, she was sure she would have been squeezed to death if she had been in the midst of the throng moving forward. Ting was surprised to see that it took only a few minutes for all those people to make their way off the airplane. She wondered if all of them were meeting people they hadn't seen in a long time, too.

"Are you Ting?"

A man wearing a shirt with the same leaf symbol the flight attendant had on her uniform was suddenly by her side. Ting was surprised when she heard and saw that he was Chinese. She had been bracing herself, thinking she would not be able to understand anything that was said to her, and here was the first Canadian she met speaking her own language! This gave her the extra courage she needed.

"Yes. Do you know where my mama and baba are?"

"One thing at a time. First you must clear through customs and immigration. That's where they will check your papers to be sure everything is in order."

At this Ting's stomach gave another lurch. Were her papers in order? Mei Yima had taken care of everything, and she was always very careful, but maybe she hadn't understood some of the instructions. Maybe she'd made a mistake.

"Don't worry! The agent will just want to check to see if you really are who your papers say you are and that your bags don't have anything forbidden, that's all. It will only take a few minutes, and then we can go to the arrival area where your parents are waiting."

When it was Ting's turn to see the immigration officer, she was surprised again. This man was also Chinese! She was just getting ready to speak to him when he turned to the co-worker standing next to him and said something in English. When he turned back to Ting, she blurted the first English word that popped into her head. "Goodbye!"

The officer looked startled, and Ting realized her mistake. She could feel her cheeks growing warm, and she kept her eyes focused down at her shoes so she wouldn't have to meet his gaze. He must think she was stupid for having said goodbye when she should have said hello.

Without a second's pause the officer said, "Hello." Then he switched to Chinese!

"Your papers say your name is Li Ting and you are coming to Canada to live. Is that correct?"

Ting's relief was immense. *Does everyone in Canada speak Chinese?* she wondered. She nodded solemnly, and then the officer went on.

"It says that your previous home was in Jinan, Shandong Province, People's Republic of China. Is that correct?"

Feeling more confident now, Ting said, "Yes, it is."

"And it says here your date of birth is December 15, 1980. Is that correct?"

Ting couldn't breathe. Her birthday was December 16, not December 15! But if she told the man this, he might tell her she could not enter the country because her papers were incorrect. She would have to fly all the way back to China, and she would not get to see Mama and Baba. She stood there silently staring at the man, panic gripping her.

The man was smiling as he said, "You have the same

birthday as my wife." Then, handing her back her passport and other papers, he said, "Welcome to Canada. *Bienvenue au Canada.*"

· Chapter 13 ·

The man with the leaf on his shirt was pulling a cart with her baggage on it. Ting held on to her small cloth bag. It made her feel more secure to hold something familiar as they walked briskly down the long hall on their way to the arrival area. Most of the other passengers had already gone. After the long plane ride with the constant hum of the engines, followed by the noise of a thousand voices all at once in the customs and immigration area, the sudden quiet was a relief to Ting's ears.

"Here you are. Your parents should be on the other side of these doors."

A set of wide doors opened automatically as Ting and her helper approached. Ting looked nervously around the huge room, wondering if it would be difficult to spot her parents among all the people hugging and crying and saying hello. She needn't have worried. There, standing right by the entrance to the waiting area, stood her mama and baba!

"Ting Ting!" two voices cried out in unison.

"Mama! Baba!"

Now they became part of that crowd of hugging,

crying people. First Mama hugged her, then Baba hugged her, then Mama hugged her again! Tears rolled down all of their cheeks, even Baba's. They all started to talk at once, then all stopped at once to hear what the other person was trying to say. This made them laugh, a sort of nervous laugh—the kind you do when things have been stressful and you laugh over silly things.

"Little Ting Ting, you're not so little anymore," Baba exclaimed.

"You seem the same size to me, Baba." At this declaration her parents both laughed, and then Mama began to speak.

"I have missed you so much! We have so many things to show you, and I want to hear how everyone back home in China is doing. Mei Yima said you have been very busy preparing for the trip to Canada."

"It was very lonely without you, Mama. Mei Yima and Shan Yifu were kind to me, though, and Bo Yima often came over to visit."

"And what about Junjie? Did you two manage not to hurt each other while you lived under the same roof?" Mama smiled as she said this. She knew how Ting felt about her spoiled cousin.

Ting was just about to say that he was an annoying pest, and that the only good thing about leaving China was to get far away from him. Then she remembered the jade panda safely tucked away in her pocket, and the strange look on Junjie's face as they said goodbye.

"We managed."

Ting took a look around her. She realized that her helper had vanished—she hadn't had a chance to thank him. Then she noticed that most of the people in the arrival area were foreigners. Her city of Jinan had only a handful of foreigners. Beijing had more, but still, in Ting's lifetime she had seen very few non-Asians. Now she was surrounded by them! It wasn't just their hair and eye colour that was different. Even the way they walked seemed foreign—all loose at the joints, swinging their arms as they went along. It was as Ting was observing these differences that it hit her. *These* people weren't the foreigners—*she* was!

Her parents led her out through sliding doors at the front of the building to a taxicab. Ting was surprised by this, since taxicabs were very expensive in China. Apparently they were expensive in Canada, too, because they took the cab only as far as a bus stop.

As the taxi crossed a big bridge, Baba explained that they were going over the Fraser River, and just past this bridge it flowed into the Pacific Ocean, the ocean Ting had just crossed on her journey.

Ting was so busy talking with her parents that she didn't look around too much at her new city until the bus pulled out and was on its way. Just like on the airplane, the first thing she noticed was the mountains. Seen from the ground, they were even more enormous! One after the other they jutted up into the sky, greenish blue until the topmost parts, where it looked as if someone had haphazardly placed giant rocks.

"You could fit a million Buddhas on those mountains!"

Her parents laughed and agreed with her. Then Baba pointed to all the skyscrapers standing like pieces on a game board and told her that was the downtown area of the city.

"There is a place called Stanley Park near those tall buildings. We'll take you there once you are settled in. Your mama and I sent you a postcard from there."

Ting thought about the card with the pictures of the totem poles carved by the native people and wasn't sure she wanted to go to that place. After the first few bus stops Ting felt her eyes grow heavy, and even though she tried her hardest to keep them open, she eventually gave up. She was just too tired. Then, all of a sudden, Mama was tapping her shoulder and telling her to wake up.

"Hurry, get your bag. Baba and I will take the suitcases. This is where we get off."

Ting looked around her, feeling dizzy and confused. Hearing Mama telling her to hurry reminded her of yesterday morning, with Mei Yima hurrying everyone around her. She shook her head in an attempt to get rid of the fuzzy feeling. Had it really been just yesterday that she was back in China?

· Chapter 14 ·

Ting looked around in confusion. She did not see any homes or apartment blocks. There were just many small, rundown businesses on the busy street. She had already noticed that streets here in Canada were very different from those in China. Instead of narrow streets crowded with bicycles going every which way, here the streets were wide, with many lines marked on them. Baba said that was so the many cars and trucks did not hit each other. They had these markings on the bigger streets in Jinan as well, but there were not so many vehicles there, and the ones that were on the road paid little attention to the lines, seeming to drive in all directions at once.

Her parents walked ahead of her, and she was very careful not to let them out of her sight. The thought of being lost in the midst of all these foreigners—Ting stopped and corrected herself—in the midst of all these *Canadians* made her stomach lurch. They stopped at a narrow opening sandwiched between two small shops. One shop sold what looked to be some kind of sweet treat with a hole in the middle, and the other shop was filled with lines and stacks of machines. Baba pulled a key out of his pocket.

"Come on, we go through here and up these stairs."

Ting followed, wondering where they could possibly be going. She noticed a stale smell the moment they stepped inside the building—an unpleasant mix of cigarette smoke and cooking grease. The carpet on the floor was old and torn, and the dirty green paint on the walls was flaking away. The stairwell leading to the upper floor was so narrow that Mama and Baba had trouble manoeuvring the suitcases through the tiny passage.

When they finally reached the top of the stairs, Ting saw a hallway that wasn't much wider than the stairwell. Two doors with numbers on them were on each side of the hall. Baba put the key in the second door on the right and opened it wide. Ting peeked inside and was confused to see it was almost empty. She looked at her parents in surprise.

Their home in China had not been large, and they certainly hadn't been rich, but it seemed like it now when she looked at this new place. In Jinan they'd had a beautiful wooden table and chairs that Yeye had made, a hand-carved chest that had been in their family for many years, and many other things that had made it feel like a home. In this room there was a dirty old brown couch, a couple of beat-up chairs, a small chest of drawers with one of the drawers missing, and a sagging bed. This was not a home. It was four walls surrounding a forlorn-looking space. It looked the way Ting was starting to feel inside.

Just then Mama said, "Come look out the window, Ting Ting. I think you'll be very surprised!"

Reluctantly Ting let herself be led over to the window. She was trying very hard not to let her parents see how disappointed she was by her new surroundings. After all, they had waited so long to be together again. She did not want to spoil it for everyone. She gasped when Mama pulled back the skimpy curtain and Ting found herself looking out onto the very first thing she had noticed about this new city of Vancouver—those beautiful mountains big enough to hold a million Buddhas.

For the first time since that moment at the airport, Ting felt happy. Looking at those mountains standing guard over the city at their feet, she felt a little less afraid.

• Chapter 15 •

When Ting woke up the next morning, she was surprised at how much better she felt. She had been so tired yesterday from her long journey that she had fallen asleep soon after dinner. The dinner itself had been a huge disappointment. The Chinese custom was to celebrate big events with a wonderful meal, one that had course after course of delicious food. So last night when Mama had served them plain rice, some fried tofu, and carrots, with an apple each for dessert, she felt very let down. Was there not good food in Canada? Did Mama not yet know where the good stalls and markets were to buy the ingredients she needed to make Ting's favourite foods, like pork dumplings, sea cucumber soup, and spicy noodles?

The first thing Ting did was to jump off the couch, which she'd discovered last night would also be serving as her bed, and run to the window to look at the mountains. Of course she knew they would still be there, but she just needed to feel their reassuring presence before she faced this first full day in her new country. Mama was making congee, and as soon as Ting finished her bowl, Mama said they would be going out to run some errands.

"We need to go to the laundry to clean our clothes, and then we will buy the things you need to start school next week."

Ting was trying her hardest not to think about school next week. When stray thoughts did manage to sneak their way into her head, she quickly pushed them back out again. The thought of going to a new school—one where they spoke English and not Chinese, one where her best friend, Yin, wouldn't be there to greet her on the first day, one where everyone would look at her and think *foreigner*—filled her with terror.

She and Mama each carried a bundle of clothes down the stairs and into the little shop Ting had noticed yesterday, the one with all the machines. In China they'd had a little washing machine in their house. Not many people were able to have one, so Mama had always told Ting how lucky they were. As Ting lugged her heavy bundle down the stairs, she began to see why Mama had considered it a luxury to have that machine right in their own home. The shop was very loud, and Mama had to raise her voice for Ting to be able to hear her. They placed the clothes and some powder in two gigantic machines. Then Mama plunked some coins in.

"We'll come back in an hour. They should be finished by then."

Next they walked down the street a few blocks until they came to a store that had a display of makeup, magazines, and notebooks in the window. Mama walked up and down the aisles, carefully looking at pencils, paper, scissors, and glue. She carried a little basket with her, and when she had inspected an item and seemed satisfied she would place it inside. When they got to the counter to pay, Mama took out her purse while she watched the lady add up the cost. When Mama saw the total she frowned, then pulled the scissors out of the pile of purchases. She used her hands to gesture that she did not want them, and the lady added up the cost again. This time when Mama saw the total she seemed satisfied and handed over some odd-looking coins.

Then they went into a small grocery store that had row after row of strange packages of food. One section had cardboard boxes stacked on the shelves, many with pictures of animals or cartoon characters on the front. Another had cans with pictures of things Ting had never seen before. Most perplexing of all was a cooler with milk at the back of the store. Of course Ting knew what milk was, but along with the regular-looking containers of milk were plastic jugs filled with a brown liquid. Could it be that cows in Canada gave brown milk as well as white?

"Mama, what is this?" she asked, pointing at the mysterious bottles.

"Baba told me it is chocolate-flavoured milk. These Canadians certainly come up with some strange ideas."

"Well," Ting said, "I didn't think cows would give brown milk. Mama, can we try some, please?"

Mama got a frown on her face and said they would buy some another time. After paying for the few small items she had picked out, she hurried Ting out of the store, saying their clothes would soon be ready. When they got to the laundry, Ting was surprised to see Mama take the clothes and put them all together in one big machine—a machine even bigger than the ones they'd just come out of. Mama then put some coins in a slot, pushed a button, and said they would come back in another hour.

"What is that thing?"

"A machine called a clothes dryer. We have no space in our small apartment to hang more than a few items at a time to dry. In Canada it's very common to have a machine dry your clothes."

Ting thought about how in Jinan, she and Mama would place the clean wet clothes on the pole that stuck out from the side of their house. That was what everyone did with their clothes. How strange that here in Canada people paid money to do what the wind and warm air could do for free.

· Chapter 16 ·

That weekend, her first in Canada, Ting's parents said they would take the bus to Stanley Park. Ting was glad they would finally be doing something that took them out of the apartment. So far Canada seemed a very dull place. There was no one for Ting to play with. There was nothing in their apartment for her to do other than use the coloured pencils and paper she had been allowed to take from the airplane, and she had long ago run out of things to draw. All of her toys and books were back home in China. *But that is not home anymore*, Ting reminded herself for the hundredth time.

One bright spot was when she remembered the writing paper Mei Yima had given her. She took it out and wrote a letter to Yin, being careful not to let her disappointment in her new country show.

Dear Yin,
I was so sad that I didn't get a chance to say goodbye to you. I knew you would be sad, too, so I asked Mei Yima if she would give you my fish to take care of. I am hoping you can keep each other from getting too lonely.

The airplane ride was very long. I sat between the window and a smelly man. There was a nice flight attendant who brought me treats. When I got to Vancouver I was so nervous I said goodbye to the immigration man instead of hello! When I finally got to see Mama and Baba we all hugged and cried.

There are gigantic mountains near the city. Two of the mountaintops look like lions, so that is what people here call them. Baba told me that one of the mountains has a car on a cable that you can ride to the top. If you ever come to visit me we will go up together.

Next to our apartment is a small shop that sells a strange-looking baked treat. They are round and have holes in the middle, just like a bicycle tire. They smell delicious. In the early morning the smell comes up into our apartment and I pretend I'm eating one with my congee. I'll let you know what they taste like once I have one.

The strangest thing of all is they have brown milk here in Canada! They put chocolate flavour in, which I think is a very good idea. I will let you know what that is like once I have it, too. Maybe I'll have a glass of the brown milk and one of the bicycle tire treats at the same time.

I hope you are well. Please write and let me know how our class at school is doing. Has Junjie been in trouble lately?

> Your friend,
> Ting

It was exciting to take the bus to Stanley Park. It took a long time, and there were many stops, but Ting didn't mind. There were so many things to see! As they made their way through the downtown core she had to put her head way back to see the tops of some of the buildings. One building had strange rope-like things on it that looked as if they were holding the building down so it wouldn't blow away in the wind.

"Those are in case of an earthquake," Baba said.

"Earthquake? You mean they have earthquakes here?" Ting asked in alarm.

"Not very often, and the city is well prepared for them if they do have them. That's why that building has been built like that. It will help it withstand any movement."

Ting looked up at the mountains and wondered what would happen to them if the ground started shaking. Fortunately she didn't have time to think about that for long, because suddenly they had arrived at the park.

Ting burst off the bus like an animal let out of a cage, and that was really what she had felt like since she got to Canada. She grabbed her parents by the hand and urged them to walk faster. It was another beautiful day, warm and sunny, and there was a smell in the air that Ting recognized. It was the ocean, and it smelled just like when they visited Qingdao. Ting could see the water to her right, along with some boats. There was a path that wound along by the water, and Ting lost no time in getting to it.

"Come on, let's go down here!"

There were many other people walking along the path, but not nearly as many people as a park would have back in China. That was something Ting had noticed right away about Canada. It seemed empty. Ting found she liked the feeling of not being in the midst of a crowd all the time. Here she felt as if she could move and breathe.

"Ting Ting," Baba said, "do you recognize those statues over there from the postcard we mailed to you?"

Remembering her fears about the native people, Ting cast an apprehensive glance to where he was pointing. Then she let out a gasp. She could not believe what she was seeing—they were beautiful! The colourful poles stood tall and proud, with all sorts of interesting things that looked like birds and other animals carved into them. Ting forgot her fears and pulled her parents along with her to get a closer look. When they got to the poles, Ting stood right underneath one and leaned way back so she could see the very top. She felt very small standing there, and she wondered how the native people could have made such a thing. Did they climb to the top of a tree and start carving it? Or did they cut down the tree first and then carve it? Ting wished she had listened more closely in Teacher Chen's class.

As they continued along the path, listening to the noisy seagulls screech overhead and the water gently lap against the retaining wall below the path, Ting was surprised when they came to a brightly carved figure jutting straight out toward the water. The reason she was so surprised was this figure looked very much like something she would see at home, with the same type of design and colours.

"It's too bad we can't read the sign telling us why this is here."

"You will soon learn enough English to understand what it says. We'll come back again and you can read it to us then."

There were some benches near the carved figure. Mama asked her if she wanted to stop and rest for a few minutes. Ting didn't want to admit it, but she *was* a bit tired from jet lag and the time change.

"If *you* are tired, Mama."

Ting immediately flopped herself down on the nearest bench. She saw her parents exchange a glance, Baba's eyes twinkling.

"Yes, my legs are a little tired," Mama said, sitting down next to her.

They sat there enjoying the light breeze on their faces and looking at all the activity in the harbour. On the other side of the water sat a gigantic bright yellow pile of something. There were many cargo ships docked, and Ting thought the colourful pile must be waiting to get loaded on one of them. Just then a huge ship—the biggest one Ting had ever seen—edged under the bright green bridge to their left.

"What do you think is on that ship, Baba?"

"People."

"People? Why would a ferry need to be so big and hold so many people?"

"It isn't a ferry. It's a cruise ship. It takes passengers on long holiday voyages up the coast of B.C. and on to Alaska."

"What is B.C.? And what is Alaska?"

"B.C. stands for British Columbia. It is the name of the province that Vancouver is in. Just like China, Canada is divided up into provinces. So now instead of being in Jinan, Shandong Province, China, you are in Vancouver, B.C., Canada."

"So what's Alaska? Another province?"

Baba laughed. "No, Alaska is a state—a part of the United States of America."

"But the United States is below Canada!"

"Yes, except for that one lonely state that sits up above our province. That's enough resting for now, and enough geography, too."

They kept walking, and soon Ting heard kids screaming and shrieking. Only it wasn't a bad kind of screaming. It was the kind that happens when kids are having fun. Sure enough, within a few minutes they saw the source of the noise. There was a large open space with lots of kids of all sizes and even some grown-ups running around. They were all soaking wet, and it was easy to see why. Suddenly water would pop up from the ground, or come shooting out of the side of one of the structures that made up the play area. Ting looked longingly at the water park, but she didn't have any dry clothes to change into. That was when Mama surprised her by reaching into her bag and pulling out a dry shirt and pair of shorts. Ting took one look, flipped off her sandals, and ran into the water.

After she had cooled off at the water park and changed into the dry clothes, they left the path along the water and cut through some tall trees. These were, in fact, the tallest trees Ting had ever seen in her life. She didn't know it was possible for trees to be so large! She wondered what a totem pole would be like if it was carved out of one of these giants.

There was a building up ahead, and once they were at the front Ting could see it was an aquarium. Ting loved aquariums! Of course, she had had her own small one in Jinan, but she had also been to a large one when they visited Qingdao. It had been her favourite part of that whole trip. A long tunnel led through the inside of the aquarium, so that you were surrounded by water on all sides and from above. Fish swam all around you, making you feel like you were really underwater.

They had spent hours at the Qingdao aquarium, and some of the smaller tanks had left Ting feeling quite hungry. She loved seafood, and seeing the jelly-fish, octopus, and especially the shrimp had made her tummy growl. Shrimp were her favourite, and she would always save the best part for last—sucking the head to get all the juices out. So when Ting saw this aquarium, she begged her parents to take her.

They entered and went up to the desk to pay. Ting

watched as her parents looked at the price list, shock registering on their faces. They stepped away from the desk, but Ting could hear them arguing quietly in the corner. She was sure they were arguing about the cost, but they kept using a strange English word—*dollars*. It sounded quite funny to hear this one English word getting thrown into the middle of sentences. Then Ting remembered something. When she had been shopping for school supplies with Mama, the lady taking the money had used the same word. *That's it!* thought Ting. *Dollars is the Canadian word for money.*

"I'm sorry, Ting Ting," said Baba. "We will have to do the aquarium another time. It's late and I think we need to head home."

Suddenly Ting didn't feel too disappointed about the aquarium. For the first time she had figured out an English word all on her own, and if she could figure out one word, she knew she could figure out more.

· Chapter 17 ·

That night Ting fell asleep the moment her head hit the pillow. The fresh air, exercise, and remnants of jet lag had left her very tired, but it was a good tired. She fell asleep thinking about gigantic trees with faces carved on them. Sometime later she woke up. At first she didn't know where she was, but then she remembered she was in their small apartment in Vancouver. Rubbing her eyes, she heard her parents speaking in harsh whispers from the bed in the corner. *That is one thing about this place*, thought Ting. *We're so crowded together I don't have to work very hard to be able to hear the grown-ups' conversations.*

"Shu, you know we do not have enough money. We cannot waste the little we do have on trivial things like an aquarium."

"It might seem trivial to you, Hai, but she's just a little girl. To Ting Ting it is important to have experiences beyond the four dull walls of this place."

"She'll have experiences soon enough. School starts in a few more days. There will be many opportunities for her once she goes there."

"But still, it would have made her so happy to go to

the aquarium. It would have reminded her of happier times. I worry about her, Hai. She looks so sad sitting for hours looking out that window at the mountains in the distance."

Baba's voice softened as he said, "You know I'm concerned for her, too. I want her happiness, but I also have to think about our finances. Now that the Chinese government is no longer paying for me to attend school and we are having to depend on the refugee money the Canadian government is giving us, it's a very difficult situation. If I could just find a job, things would be so much better."

"I know you love her, Hai. You just need to remember what it is like to be a child. And I know you'll find a job soon."

"Don't be too sure about that, Shu. My English is very poor, and my qualifications from China will not be accepted here. Nor, for that matter, will yours."

There were a few more words spoken after that, but Ting could not make out what they were. It was just as well. What she had heard was more than enough to think about. Now she understood why Mama had decided not to buy the scissors that day at the store, and why she didn't get to go to the aquarium. It also explained why there had been no pork dumplings or other good food when she arrived. Why, night after night, they ate the same thing—rice, tofu, and a few vegetables. Those foods were cheap and their family was now poor. The last thought Ting had before sleep claimed her again was *And what does it mean that Baba and Mama's qualifications are not accepted in Canada?*

• • •

School was due to start on Tuesday. Monday was a holiday called Labour Day. By the end of it Ting decided holidays here in Canada were very strange. There had been no colourful parades, no crowds of people in the parks, no special meals. It seemed very dull compared to a Chinese holiday.

Since their trip to Stanley Park, Ting had been paying more attention when she was out shopping with Mama. She had managed to figure out a few more words like *please, excuse me, no,* and *yes.* It wasn't much, but it was a start. Baba spoke a little bit of English, but most of what he knew was technical language used for his courses and of no use for practical, everyday things. He'd been too busy with his studies to take the extra time needed to learn conversational English, and he had expected to return to China soon so that it wouldn't be necessary. Mama didn't seem to know many more words than Ting, so she had recently signed up for a night school class to learn more.

None of this was in time to help them figure out Ting's schooling, though. There were some very kind people at the refugee society who had helped Ting's parents when they first decided to stay in Canada. Now one of the ladies from that centre came to their apartment to help them sort out what they needed to know for the first day of school. She had emigrated from China ten years earlier, so she knew how difficult it could be to adjust.

After having a cup of green tea, she pulled out some papers from her bag. She went over items such as school hours, holidays, and the school supplies Ting would need on her first day. Mama looked alarmed when she saw the lengthy list. When they had gone shopping the previous week, she had purchased what would have been necessary for a classroom in China. There were so many more things on this list!

"What are all these things they say to buy?" she asked the lady.

The lady must have noticed Mama's distress, because she immediately said, "Don't worry if you can't get everything on this list. There are extra supplies available at the school for those students who haven't been able to get everything." Then, knowing the importance of saving face, the lady continued, "The teacher will understand that it is difficult to make such purchases when you do not yet speak English."

Mama's face relaxed at those words. After hearing her parents arguing the night before, Ting knew the reason Mama looked worried wasn't because of the English, although that was a difficulty. No, the problem was they did not have enough money to buy all these things. The lady then told them she would walk them over to the school and show Ting where her new classroom was. While they were walking over to the school, Ting suddenly thought of something.

"Where do I get my school uniform?"

Smiling down at her, the lady said, "There's no need to worry about that. In Canada students at public schools do not wear uniforms. Only students who go to private schools wear uniforms here."

Ting thought this was very strange. She had always worn a uniform to school. All children in China wore uniforms to school. This brought up a new worry for her. If she didn't have a uniform to wear, then what *would* she wear? She owned very few clothes, and most of what she did have had been left in Jinan. There had been more important things to put in her suitcase— things like Yeye's photo album, Mama's tea set, and the little wooden jewellery box that Yeye had made for her. Worry piled on more worries, making Ting wish she did not have to go to school the next day, making her wish she could get on a plane and fly back to their little house in Jinan.

·Chapter 18·

Ting was too nervous the next morning to eat even one bite of her breakfast. Mama fussed over her, saying she needed to eat to keep her strength up for the long day ahead.

Well, it's going to be a long day, all right, thought Ting. She tried to eat some of the congee just so Mama would stop hounding her, but it was no use. Neither Ting nor her stomach was eager to face what lay ahead.

Always before on the first day of school, Ting would meet Yin along the way and they would walk together, excitedly discussing what the new year might bring. Now Ting would be walking to school by herself. Well, not really by herself. Mama was going to go with her on this first day, but Ting wasn't sure this was such a good idea. She was sure that here in Canada it would be the same as in China. Eight-, soon to be nine-year-old girls did not get walked to school by their mamas. For once, Ting's stubbornness did not pay off. There was no persuading Mama to let her go by herself.

When they arrived at the school, it seemed so different from the day before, when they had been given the tour by the kind lady from the refugee society. Then it had been quiet and peaceful, with only a few adults walking around getting things ready for the first day of school. Now it was like an explosion of noise and colour and kids. The school day had not yet begun, so the playground and front space were swarming with children. Little, big, and in-between sizes of kids with hair and eyes and clothes of such a variety of colours that it almost made Ting dizzy. She was used to order in both behaviour and clothing at school. This sight shocked her!

She could see Mama was unnerved by the action going on around them, too, and for a few minutes Ting actually thought Mama might take her hand and lead her back to their apartment. But suddenly a man appeared at their side, shaking Mama's hand and smiling down at Ting. He indicated they should follow him. Once they were inside the school doors, things grew quiet, the way they always did when Ting would close the front door of their little house, shutting out the noise coming from the street.

This man looked Chinese, but the words coming out of his mouth made no sense.

"What is he saying, Mama?"

"He is speaking Cantonese."

Mama tried to speak to him in Mandarin, but the man looked as puzzled as they had when he was talking to them. Cantonese was spoken in Hong Kong, but not in most of mainland China. They were not the same language at all!

"Someone from the school must have asked for a translator for us, without realizing that not all spoken Chinese is the same."

Ting's stomach was starting to feel upset again. What would they do if they couldn't get anyone to understand them? Soon the other children would be coming in, and the thought of standing there, lonely and lost in the middle of all those faces, made Ting want to cry.

"Wait!"

Ting looked up at Mama and saw she was pulling a small notebook and a pen out of her bag.

"Cantonese and Mandarin are mostly the same when written. Even if we can't understand what the other is saying, if we write down our message the other will be able to read it."

With that Mama started madly writing away on her paper. When she handed the sheet to the man, he smiled and wrote something back. This went on for several more minutes while Ting watched, and then the man indicated they should follow him. He took them down a long hallway and stopped in front of a door with the Arabic number four on it. Ting thought she had better remember the number so she could find this room on her own the following day. She felt a flood of gratitude that at least something looked familiar to her, having worked hard on learning her numbers and math symbols all week. Math was something Baba *could* teach her in English, so they had sat together every night going over it.

The man cleared his throat and an older lady sitting at a desk at the front of the room looked up. The man then began speaking in English to the woman, who smiled at Ting as he was talking. She got up from her desk, walked over to Ting and Mama, and gave them each a big smile. For the first time that day Ting found herself relaxing. This must be her teacher, and Ting thought that anyone with such a warm smile must be all right.

Ting's new teacher shook Mama's hand just as a loud buzzer sounded. The teacher looked at them, gestured that it was time for class to begin, and hurried back to her desk. The man then led Mama away, and suddenly Ting was left standing there alone.

Students rushed past Ting, some with big backpacks still on their shoulders, others dragging them along by the straps. She felt invisible, with students going around her on both sides but seeming not to even notice her presence. When everyone was settled at a desk, she was left standing there by herself, feeling totally lost and confused.

Then, surprising Ting because she came up from behind, a girl grabbed her hand and directed Ting to an empty desk next to hers. Ting looked at the girl and thought, *Her hair has no colour. It's like someone forgot to add it in.* She gave the girl a shy smile, then quickly settled into her new place, hoping her stomach would soon do the same.

· Chapter 19 ·

Ting's first morning of school in this new country of hers passed by in a blur. A blur of sights, activities, and especially sounds. All around her were voices, but she had no idea what they were saying. Once or twice she thought she heard words she recognized, but it was all spoken so fast there was no way to know for sure. By the time the buzzer rang for lunch, Ting's head had started to ache from the strain.

She looked around as the students rushed out the door before the buzzer had even stopped. Then she looked at her teacher, expecting her to sharply reprimand the class for being so disorderly. Never would Teacher Chen have allowed such unruly behaviour! However, this teacher didn't even glance up to see what all the noise and confusion was about. She seemed to be in a hurry herself to get her things gathered up and leave for lunch. As she walked by Ting, she noticed her still sitting at her desk and called ahead to the girl who had directed Ting to her seat earlier. She said a few words to her, then went out the door.

The girl turned around and walked back to Ting. She smiled at her, then pointed to the backpack she was holding. She pointed first at Ting and then back to her backpack. Ting shook her head no. She did not have a backpack. The little girl then reached into her bag and pulled out a smaller, bright red bag from inside. Putting her hand in that, she pulled out some bread with things stuck inside, an apple, and a little package. *Of course*, Ting thought, *she wants me to get my lunch.*

Ting reached into her desk and pulled out the small, rumpled paper bag Mama had sent with her that morning. She stood and held it up to show she understood. Then the girl led her out the door and back down the long hall Ting had come through that morning until they arrived at a set of large doors.

When the girl with no hair colour pushed open the heavy doors, Ting stopped in her tracks. The noise seemed even louder in this large room than it had been that morning outside the school building, if such a thing was possible. The girl walked on a few steps before noticing Ting was not beside her. She came back and grabbed her hand again, leading her through a maze of kids, lunches, and tables that left Ting's mind reeling. She started the thought, *Back home in China* ...then stopped. *I have to stop comparing everything to China. I don't live in China anymore. I must get used to the way things are done here in Canada.*

As soon as they sat down, the girl pointed to herself and carefully said her name: "Hannah." Then she pointed at Ting and lifted her eyebrows in a questioning manner. Ting couldn't help smiling at this friendly girl. She said her name, and then the girls each pulled out their lunches. Ting had a small container of rice, an apple, and a hard-boiled egg. She frowned when she saw the apple and the egg. There had been too many of those since she arrived. However, the frown quickly disappeared when she noticed several White Rabbit candies at the bottom of her bag. Then she looked over and watched Hannah take her food out of that bright red bag. *Apples must be popular here in Canada*, she thought as she saw the first item emerge. Next came that odd bread with something stuck inside. Hannah pointed to it and then to Ting's candies. She made a switching motion with her hands.

Ting hesitated. She knew Hannah wanted to trade, but she thought, *What if I don't like whatever is stuck inside that bread?* She would be forced to chew and swallow it anyway. If she didn't, she would insult this girl who had been so nice to her. Hoping she wouldn't be sorry, she reached down and handed half of the White Rabbit candies to Hannah. Hannah handed her half of her bread in exchange.

Ting wasn't sure what to do with the bread concoction, so she watched Hannah. It appeared there was no special way to eat this thing; Hannah had simply taken a bite off one end, so Ting did the same.

"Mmm," she said without really meaning to. Inside the bread was some kind of white sauce, lettuce, some kind of meat, and a slice of cheese. It was surprisingly good! Then Hannah unwrapped one of Ting's candies, popped it in her mouth, and mimicked Ting's "mmm" verdict. They looked at each other and laughed. It felt like a year since Ting had laughed. It was a good feeling.

· Chapter 20 ·

Later that night, as Ting lay on the couch trying to fall asleep, she couldn't stop thinking about her first school day in Canada. Other than feeling lonely and lost when she first arrived, it had all gone much better than she had ever dreamed possible. First, there was the girl with no hair colour, Hannah. She had been very kind to Ting, and at the end of the school day she had walked out of the classroom with her and said goodbye. She had given Ting a warm smile when Ting had said goodbye in return.

There had been two big surprises that afternoon, one for the teacher and one for Ting. The teacher's surprise happened during math class, right after lunch. Mrs. McBride—Ting had worked hard to remember the teacher's name—instructed everyone to get their math books out of their desks. Ting opened hers and was pleasantly surprised to see that, thanks to Baba's tutoring, she understood most of what was in front of her. Mrs. McBride then wrote out a series of problems on the board at the front of the class and asked a question. Ting could see the students around her all look away quickly, and she guessed that the teacher had asked for a volunteer to go to the front of the class to work out some of the problems.

Ting looked at the board and thought to herself, *Those are baby problems. I learned how to do those two years ago!*

Without actually meaning to, Ting raised her hand. Mrs. McBride looked surprised, but she covered her reaction quickly. Holding a piece of chalk out to Ting, she signalled for her to come to the front of the class. All of a sudden Ting felt nervous. She hadn't even liked going to the front of the class back in Jinan where she knew her classmates, and now she was going to have to go up in front of all these strangers. Every face was turned toward her, watching curiously to see what would happen.

Ting slowly walked forward and reached out a hand for the chalk. Her confidence grew as she turned her back on the class and faced the board. In no time at all she completed every problem, then turned and handed the chalk back to the teacher. Again, she noticed surprise on Mrs. McBride's face. Ting had no idea what was said to her, other than she thought she heard the words "thank you." She smiled shyly at the teacher and returned to her seat.

Ting's surprise did not happen in the classroom, but rather outside the school building. After their math class the buzzer had gone off again. It was confusing trying to figure out what all the buzzers were for, but this time Ting wasn't left to wonder very long.

Hannah came over to Ting and indicated they were to go back outside.

When they got there, Ting saw that it was some sort of exercise time. In China the students would all line up in rows and do calisthenics together. Such order did not seem to exist here. A whistle blew. Ting looked over to see Mrs. McBride standing there holding a huge canvas bag. Students rushed up to her as she dumped the contents of the bag out on the ground. Bright yellow and red sticks scattered at her feet.

She had two students, one boy and one girl, stand next to her. Then they started calling out what Ting thought had to be names, pointing to a person at the same time. That person would go stand next to them. This went on and on, the boy and girl taking turns picking students to make up what Ting figured out were going to be two teams. It was no surprise to Ting that she was the last person to be picked. She wondered if Junjie had somehow managed to let them know in Canada how bad she was at sports! The boy had last pick, and when he saw Ting was his only choice he just turned and sighed.

Mrs. McBride then handed a red stick to the boy and a yellow stick to the girl. When the teams saw that colours had been chosen, there was a mad dash to grab the remaining sticks. Ting bent down and picked up a red stick, holding it gingerly in her hands, wondering what on earth she was supposed to do with it. She didn't have to wonder long, as she heard the whistle blow again. Looking at the large paved area she could see that a net had been set up at each end. Each net had a student with a stick fatter than the others standing in front to guard it.

Suddenly there was movement all around her. Feet were pounding and voices were yelling in excitement. The sticks slapping on the pavement made a sharp sound, and everyone seemed to be trying to hit some kind of plastic disc the teacher had thrown on the ground.

Clearly the object is to get the disc in the net, Ting thought as she observed what was happening around her.

Suddenly the disc stopped right in front of Ting's feet. She gasped in surprise. In her excitement to get the disc in the net, she did the first thing that came to mind. She picked it up and threw it directly at the person with the big stick. She realized her mistake the minute she saw the expression on the face of the boy who had sighed when he had to pick her for his team. She had seen the same look of disgust on Junjie's face countless times over the years.

It was at that moment, one that could have been a moment of humiliation and shame, that Mrs. McBride walked up to her and patted her on the back. Smiling, she took Ting's stick and showed her how to hold it. Then she took Ting over to the side of the play area and had her practise hitting an extra disc she produced from her pocket. The first time Ting connected with the disc she felt a sense of accomplishment. Mrs. McBride then pointed to the stick and said the word *stick*. Ting repeated this. Then she pointed to the disc and said *puck*. Next she did a wide sweeping motion with her arm and said the word *hockey*.

Ting rejoined the group of students playing, and within moments the puck found its way to her again. This time she hit the puck as hard as she could with her stick and watched in amazement as it sailed right past the player with the big stick and into the yellow team's net. Her teammates looked at her in shock and, Ting thought, with respect. Then they all cheered!

I think I like this sport called hockey, she told herself as they gathered up the sticks and headed back into the classroom. *I wonder if they play it very often here in Canada.*

· Chapter 21 ·

The next few weeks seemed to fly by. On the rainy days, which Ting noticed came frequently, she would hurry home from school and into their apartment. Their living space was even drearier than usual on these soggy days. The dampness made the entranceway smell worse than it normally did, and the dark skies cast a gloom into all corners of their apartment. Worst of all, when Ting would look out the window at her mountains, it was as though they had vanished into thin air. Instead of their high jagged peaks outlining the city, all she could see was grey. Grey skies, grey buildings ... even the people seemed dark and dismal with their black umbrellas opened to ward off the rain.

On the pleasant days, when the sun was shining and the sky was blue, Ting would take her time walking home. She was feeling a little less lonely than when she'd first arrived in Canada. She now knew the full name of the girl with no hair colour. It was Hannah Larsson. She and Hannah spent time together during the school day, but when school was over Hannah's mom picked her up and Ting didn't see her again until the next morning.

When Ting reached the block where she lived, she liked to look in the windows of some of the shops. Her favourite window was the one right next to the entrance to their apartment building, the one where they sold those baked goods with the holes in them. Ting had noticed that some people went into the shop, bought one or two, and hurried back out again. Others would buy one along with a drink and sit down to enjoy their treat. The smell that wafted out as customers went in and out the door was almost more than she could bear.

After several days the owner noticed her standing with her nose stuck against the window and motioned for her to come inside. Ting desperately wanted to go into that shop, but she knew she didn't have any money to buy one of the treats. She shook her head politely, then turned and went to the apartment. She did not go to the window again for a few days for fear the man would see her and want her to come in to buy something.

Ting had a sweet tooth, though, and the smells soon had her back at the window watching the customers make their purchases. She kept an eye out for the owner, planning to slip away quickly if she saw him head her way. So she was taken by surprise when he appeared right behind a group of customers walking out the door with their bags of treats. This time the man did not motion her inside. Instead, to Ting's surprise and delight, he handed her one of the treats with a hole in the middle! Ting hesitated, but only for a moment. She reached out and took the offering, and with a huge smile on her face she said, "Thank you."

The man smiled back and pointed at the treat. "Doughnut."

With that he turned and walked back into his shop. Ting looked at this thing called a doughnut that she was holding in her hand. It was soft and warm, and the sugar crystals coating it felt crunchy beneath her fingers. She nibbled off one small bite and started chewing, half afraid that its flavour would not be as good as its smell. But she was wrong! Before she knew it, her hands were empty. She had eaten the whole thing!

School was good and bad at the same time. There had been that glorious moment on the first day when she had scored a goal while playing hockey. Now when teams were picked, hers was no longer the last name called. *Maybe my parents gave me the right name after all*, she thought. In China, names often had meanings assigned to them, and Ting's meant "graceful." *Wouldn't Junjie be surprised if he could see me play this game called hockey? I bet I could even score a goal on him!*

After that first day there was a two-hour block every morning when Ting was taken to a different classroom, one with students of all ages and sizes sitting in it. This was the special class for students who did not speak English. Ting's stubbornness pushed her to work harder than everyone else in this class. She was determined to learn English as soon as possible. Although the teacher was very kind and patient, going to the special class made her feel stupid, and she did not like that feeling at all.

Most of the students in her regular class seemed kind enough, but there were a handful who enjoyed teasing her about her attempts to speak English. The first time it happened was after Ting had called out the teacher's name during class because she was having trouble understanding a word.

She could hear a few kids giggle when they heard her pronunciation, but the teacher quickly silenced them all with one stern look. After that the giggling, pointing, and teasing only happened when they were well out of the range of Mrs. McBride's sharp ears, during recess and the lunch hour. Most of those times she was with her new friend Hannah, and that kept them silent, but on days when Hannah was home sick or had to stay inside to finish an assignment, Ting suffered the humiliation of being ridiculed.

But Ting's reaction was only to study her English even harder. She was used to teasing. After all, she had Junjie as a cousin. What she was *not* used to was not being a top student. She knew that until she mastered this new language, she would not be able to learn as much as the others in her class. Yes, she was already the top math student, but there were so many other subjects, such as science and history, where she was completely at a loss.

Still, the teasing did hurt. One day Ting was in the bathroom, and when she went to the sink to wash her hands she saw soap dribbled all over the counter. Out of habit from her school in China, Ting grabbed a paper towel and started cleaning off the counter. Two girls came into the bathroom at that moment and started pointing and laughing at her. Their words were spoken so fast that Ting didn't understand most of what they said, but she did catch some words, including *foreigner* and *stupid*. Humiliated, she walked back to her classroom with her head hanging down.

Then there was today. Just thinking about it made Ting's stomach feel icky. Yesterday Mama had come to meet her at the end of the school day. When Ting walked out of the building, she and Mama had naturally called out greetings to each other. She had heard several students snicker but had no idea what they thought was so funny.

In the morning when she arrived at school, she heard a group of kids saying, "Where is your mama, Ting-Ting-a-ling? Only babies have mamas! Shouldn't you be home with your mama, little baby Ting Ting?"

In confusion Ting had walked on, pretending not to notice them. Inside, however, she was raging. How dare they make fun of her mama! And what was wrong with *Ting Ting*? It had never occurred to her to be embarrassed about her nickname. When she met up with Hannah, she explained what had happened as best she could in her broken English.

Hannah looked at her sympathetically and then explained, "In Canada, *mama* is what a baby or very small child calls their mother. *Mom* would be what anyone older would use. And I guess *Ting Ting* sounds like a bell, so that seems funny to kids here. But what they did was really mean."

Now Ting understood—the Chinese word for mother sounded like a babyish word for mother in English! But understanding this didn't keep her from a different kind of trouble she suddenly found herself in.

· Chapter 22 ·

When Ting arrived home from school, Mama asked her if she wanted to walk to the local grocer's with her to pick up some vegetables and fruit. Still stinging from the morning's ridicule, Ting made up her mind. This was Canada, and from now on she was going to work hard at being a Canadian on the outside, even if she still felt Chinese on the inside.

"No, Mom, I have homework to do."

There was a long moment of silence. Then a mini-explosion.

"*What* did you just call me?" Mama asked indignantly.

"*Mom*. It's what kids in Canada call their mothers." Ting could see the set look in Mama's eyes and knew she was in for a battle. Mama could be every bit as stubborn as Ting.

"This might be Canada, but I am your *mama*. I do not want you calling me by this Canadian name."

"But it's what kids here say. You can't expect me to live here and act like I'm still in China!"

Ting was on the verge of tears. All the frustration, loneliness, and exhaustion she had experienced since she arrived bubbled to the surface and came pouring out. Before she could stop the words they were out of her mouth. "I didn't ask to come here. I did not want to come here. It's your and Baba's fault. You've taken me away from my home, and now you ask me not to fit in here in my new home. I hate you!"

Of course, Ting did not mean the horrid words that came out. Not the part about hating her mama, anyway. But it was too late. They had been spoken and there was no way to take them back, to undo the hurt she could see on her mama's face. Even worse, it was only because she hated being teased so much that she had decided to try using the word *Mom*. Deep down, she liked *Mama* much better.

The rest of the day passed in complete silence, at least until Baba arrived home from the meeting he had been attending. Then Mama motioned for him to go outside the apartment with her. Sometime later they both came back, Baba now wearing the same serious expression as Mama.

Dinner was eaten with very few words spoken, and afterwards Ting immediately started doing the rest of her homework, even though it was almost impossible to keep her mind on the words in front of her. When she was done, she brushed her teeth, put her pajamas on, and made up her bed on the old couch. It was the first time Ting had ever gone to bed without a good-night hug from Mama and Baba, or when they were gone, Yima. She thought it might be the loneliest feeling ever—way lonelier than not having friends or not being

114

able to communicate with people. Sighing sadly, she closed her eyes, but sleep would not come. She couldn't help overhearing her parents' quiet conversation.

"Shu, you know Ting didn't mean what she said."

"I know, Hai, but maybe this is too hard for her. Maybe we made a mistake in deciding to bring her to Canada."

"We still don't know if it is safe for me to return. What choice do we have?"

"She could have stayed with her yimas in Jinan."

Ting heard Mama start crying and Baba speaking words too soft for Ting to understand. Then she heard Mama speak.

"It's hard for all of us, maybe Ting most of all. We must do what we can to help her adjust."

Relief flooded Ting when she realized Mama knew she hadn't meant the awful things she had said. That was all it took for her to finally be able to fall asleep.

The next morning Mama acted as if nothing had happened. When it was time for Ting to leave for school, Mama handed her the brown paper lunch bag filled, no doubt, with the usual rice, egg, and apple. As Ting turned to leave, she heard Mama speak.

"Aren't you going to give your mom a hug before you go to school?"

Ting could not believe her ears! She dropped her lunch and books on the floor and ran to Mama, hugging her tightly.

"Thank you, Mama, I mean Mom." And she headed to school, feeling just a little bit more Canadian than she had the day before.

· Chapter 23 ·

By the time October rolled around, Ting was beginning to feel more comfortable in her new surroundings. She had scored several more goals in hockey, and Hannah had told her about an even better version of the game—one played on ice. Ting desperately wanted to see this. She tried to imagine skaters zooming around with the puck, and sticks banging the ice as they glided along. *It must be awesome!* she had thought, remembering the English word of praise she'd often heard on the playground.

While her parents, especially Mama, struggled with their English, Ting was learning the language at an amazing rate. Mr. Long, the teacher she had for her ESL (English as a Second Language) class, was very pleased and had told her that by the end of November she probably wouldn't need to attend the class anymore. Ting planned to do all she could to make his prediction come true.

Ting hadn't thought there could be anything more exciting to discover in their neighbourhood than those delicious doughnuts, but she had been wrong. Mr. Long told Ting she now knew enough English that she could benefit from getting a membership at the local public library. Ting had looked at him blankly. He had gone on to explain how each area of the city had a place where you could go to borrow books. Ting had never been to a building filled with nothing but books, and she thought it sounded like a wonderful place. You were allowed to take them home for a few weeks, then return them and check out more. And best of all—it was free! During one of the ESL classes he took the students on a trip to the local library, showed them how to use it, and helped each one get a library card.

The moment Ting entered the library, a happy feeling started somewhere near her toes and worked its way up to the top of her head. There were books *everywhere*—rows and rows of them, shelf after shelf, filling the whole building! Mr. Long showed them the section with children's books and suggested they start with some of the books for younger kids, since those had only a few words on each page. When he saw the insulted looks on their faces, he assured them that in no time at all they would be ready for the books that were meant for their own age group.

As they were looking around the shelves, trying to make the tough decisions of which books they should check out, Ting's eyes fell upon a display in the corner. Several books stood propped up on the counter, and in the middle of them was a miniature house. The house was what first caught her attention. It was a very strange-looking house, not like anything Ting had seen before. It was made out of logs instead of wood or bricks or stone. Curious, she wandered over to have a closer look.

The little house made of logs was open at the front so you could see inside. The bottom had just two rooms—one a big, open space with a stone fireplace against the wall, the other a tiny bedroom in the back left corner. A small table with four chairs sat near the fireplace, and there was a rocking chair nearby as well. The upstairs was an open loft with a ladder extending up and peeking through. The loft floor was covered with a colourful braided rug, and there was a bed in the middle of the room.

Ting was entranced by the display and wondered about the books set up around the tiny house. She went to ask Mr. Long if she could borrow one of them.

He looked over to where she was pointing and smiled. "Those are very famous books, Ting. They are by an author named Laura Ingalls Wilder, who wrote about what it was like to grow up in North America over a hundred years ago."

"Please, may I get book?" She just knew they were for her. "*Please?*"

Mr. Long looked at her, and she could see the indecision on his face. How could she convince him? Then she had a sudden inspiration. She quickly ran over, grabbed one, and headed back to him. Opening to the first page she slowly, hesitantly, started reading.

"Once upon a time, sixty years ago, a l-l-little girl lived in the Big Woods of Wis... Wis..."

Ting got stuck on this word and looked up at Mr. Long.

"Wisconsin," he filled in for her. Then, seeming to make a decision, he took the book from her hands.

Ting held her breath as she watched to see what he would do with it. With relief she saw him look through its pages, smiling several times as he came upon some of the illustrations, then hand the book back to her.

"This will be a very good reading lesson for you. Each day I want you to spend some time reading, and every time you come to a word you can't read, or even if you *can* read it but don't know what it means, write it down and bring it to class with you. We will go over it together. This book is called *Little House in the Big Woods*. It is the first of many books this author has written, so if you like this one, you can check out more when you are finished."

Ting hugged the book to her and gave her teacher a huge smile. "Thank you!"

Ting had no way of knowing it in that moment, but that book would prove to be the key to propelling her out of Mr. Long's ESL class by the end of November, just as he had predicted.

· Chapter 24 ·

Shortly after the trip to the library, Ting started to hear talk of something called *Halloween*. She asked Hannah what this word meant.

"It's a sort of holiday, but not one you get off school."

"Oh, great," said Ting, "another holiday like that... Labour Day."

At this Hannah burst out laughing. "No! It's nothing like Labour Day. Halloween is on the last day of October, and that night kids get to dress up in costumes and go around to houses in their neighbourhood trick or treating."

"What?" Ting asked, at a loss.

"When the person comes to the door, you say 'Trick or treat!' The idea is that they give you a candy or some other treat. If they don't, you can play a trick on them, but nobody really does the trick part anymore. I think that happened a long time ago when Halloween first started."

"Can anyone do this?"

"Sure. You just have to put on some kind of costume and take a bag with you to hold all the candy you get. Oh—and you want one of your parents to go with you, of course." Hannah hesitated for a minute, then continued. "You might want to work on saying 'trick or treat' before you go, though."

A day when you could go door to door and ask for candy? This sounded almost too good to be true. Maybe Canada's holidays weren't *all* terrible after all! Then Ting thought about what Hannah had just said about needing to practise saying "trick or treat." She was right, of course. Ting was learning English very quickly, but there were still many words that were difficult for her to say. She loved candy, though! She would work harder than ever on her new language. She was determined to have it right by this day called Halloween. The bigger problem would be convincing her parents to let her participate.

• • •

Several times since Ting had arrived in Canada, people from the refugee society had come by. Sometimes it was just to talk with her parents, and other times it was to deliver a bag of clothes or some kitchen items they thought might be useful. Ting could tell it was hard for her parents to accept these things, that it made them feel like beggars. But she also knew from having listened to many late-night discussions that their financial situation was not good. It was a loss of face to accept this charity, but they had no choice.

One day when Ting returned home from school, right after eating another one of the doughnuts the owner, Mr. Dabrowski, had given her, she entered the apartment and found two older ladies from the refugee society sitting at the table sharing tea with Mama. Mama looked relieved to see her.

"Ting, come say hello to these ladies. They have brought us some clothes, and they have something mysterious in a box they keep smiling and pointing to. I can't understand much else." She then introduced the women, a Mrs. Smith and a Mrs. Endicott.

Ting smiled at the ladies, then watched as they pulled an object out of a large cardboard box. She gasped when she saw what it was.

"A TV!"

Mama's eyes also grew large when she saw what the ladies had brought them. In China they'd had a small black-and-white TV, and it had been considered quite a luxury. She turned to Ting and asked her to explain to the ladies that they could not accept such an expensive gift.

Ting looked at Mama, horrified. In rapid Chinese she proceeded to tell her mother how great this would be for their English. They could watch Canadian programming and learn way more quickly than they were able to right now. Ting begged her to let them keep the TV, and she could see by the look on Mama's face that she was wavering. She made one last attempt. "Mama, think of how much this will help Baba. Once he can speak English well enough, surely someone will want to hire him for a job."

As Ting had hoped, that was enough to convince Mama. She told Ting to tell the ladies that they would accept the gift with gratitude.

Yippee! thought Ting in English. She felt only the tiniest twinge of guilt for saying they needed the TV for Baba, when what she really wanted was to be able to watch hockey played on ice. Bursting with happiness she turned to the two ladies and addressed them in the traditional Chinese way of showing great respect.

"Thank you, Old Smith and Old Endicott."

The two women looked shocked, but then they glanced at each other and burst out laughing. When they recovered enough to be able to speak, they gently explained to Ting that in this country, unlike China, it was not considered polite to address someone as old—that, in fact, it was quite the opposite. It was a good thing they were used to working with immigrants! No harm was done, and the TV stayed.

Not long after the wonderful day the TV was delivered, another visitor came to their door. This time it was a man. His knocking was so loud it actually made Mama jump. Baba went to the door, cracking it open to see who was on the other side.

Of course, Ting's curiosity meant she was standing right behind Baba, trying to look around him to see who could possibly be there to visit them. The only people who had ever come to their door had been from the refugee society, and they never came on a Saturday.

"Hello," the man said. "Do you mind if I come on in and put this in your fridge?"

Ting could see that the visitor was holding two bags, and from the looks of it one was obviously quite heavy. It was sagging down almost to the ground and the man seemed to be sagging, too—probably from having lugged whatever it was up all those stairs.

Baba stared at the man without replying. Ting was desperate to see what was in the bags, especially that big one, so she spoke up from behind Baba.

"Yes, please. I show you fridge."

She scooted in front of Baba and opened the door for the man, then led him into the kitchen. Once he put down the heavy bag, he was able to catch his breath again. He extended a hand and pumped Baba's enthusiastically.

"Hi. I'm Mark Thompson. I volunteer with the Salvation Army. The refugee society hands us a list of names every year of people who are celebrating their first Thanksgiving here in Canada. We like to make up food hampers with all the fixings for a nice Thanksgiving meal and deliver them to any of the families who might like one."

The words came out in such a rush that Ting had a hard time understanding them all. But one look at her parents' faces and she knew she had comprehended way more than they had. She turned to Mama and Baba and quickly told them what the man had said, hoping she hadn't missed anything important. Then she turned back to Mr. Thompson.

"My parents and I thank you. You are kind."

"You're welcome. I think you will enjoy what the volunteers have put together."

After more talking between Ting and her parents,

she turned back to the man and said, "My mom say thank you again."

"No problem, it's just the basic Thanksgiving fare— pumpkin, cranberries, yams, Brussels sprouts. Oh, and of course a turkey!"

Ting wasn't sure what all these things were, but she smiled politely at the man and said thanks once more. He then said he had to be going, that he had several more hampers to deliver.

It wasn't until Ting closed the door that she realized something. Something very important, something she wasn't even aware of until it was over. "I, Li Ting, the girl who just two months ago said goodbye instead of hello to the man at the airport, was translating for that man and my parents!"

Still feeling proud of herself, Ting joined her parents, who were already looking in the bags Mr. Thompson had left. They pulled out a can with an orange wrapper that said it was something called pumpkin. There were two bags, one filled with bright red berries—obviously the cranberries he had mentioned. The other had round green things that looked like miniature cabbages. Mama opened the bag for them to smell, and they all agreed that yes, they had to be some kind of cabbage, but they wondered why they were so small. Finally, at the very bottom of the bag was something familiar—six huge yams, bigger than any Ting had seen before.

"They seem to have the sizes of things really mixed up here, don't they?"

Then Mama reached into the other bag—the one the man had struggled to get into their kitchen. Baba helped her, and together they pulled out a gigantic frozen lump. Ting read the label, which said "turkey." She had heard about turkeys when they talked about Thanksgiving at school, but she had never actually seen one. It was the size of six chickens put together! And then she heard her parents start to laugh.

"I guess you were right about the sizes being all confused here in Canada, Ting Ting!" Baba exclaimed.

Then they were *all* laughing. Mama laughed so hard she was wiping the tears off her cheeks. Ting looked at Mama and realized something else, something maybe even more important than the fact she had just translated between English and Chinese. This was the first time Ting had seen Mama laugh—at least the deep-down "starts at your toes" kind of laugh that you just can't stop—since she had arrived in Canada. Somehow it filled her heart with hope.

When Mama was finally able to talk she said, "Whatever are we going to do with such a big bird?"

The three of them looked at each other—and then suddenly Ting had an idea. It was the Chinese custom when given a gift to give a gift in return. Almost every day after school Mr. Dabrowski had a doughnut ready to give to her. In fact, the only days he *didn't* give her a doughnut were the days when the weather was so terrible and rainy that Ting went straight into their apartment instead of making her usual rounds of window shopping. She had been trying to think of something she could give Mr. Dabrowski in return but had been stuck for an idea. And she didn't dare ask Mama for ideas or she would find out about all the doughnuts Ting had been eating.

"Mama, why don't we give the turkey to the man who has the doughnut shop? He has been very nice to us. Remember the time we couldn't find our apartment key and he let us sit in his shop until Baba came home? And how he brought us each a doughnut to eat while we waited and then wouldn't let us pay?"

"You are very smart, Ting Ting! That's just what we will do. Hai, do you think you two could get that thing down to the doughnut shop?"

As she and Baba returned from their delivery, Ting thought things could not get any better that day. Her English skills were improving at a rapid rate. Mama had laughed so hard she had cried. It had felt good to laugh with her mama and baba. It was like back when they lived in Jinan together. There had also been the debt repaid to the doughnut man. It was Saturday, and they now had a little TV to watch a program called *Hockey Night in Canada* on, and Monday was a holiday, which meant no school.

Ting had all these happy thoughts swirling in her mind as she went to go sit by the window with her library book and work on her reading. Just as she opened the book, there was another loud knock at the door. The second time that day! Baba went to see who could possibly be standing on the other side this time, and Ting quickly followed.

"Mr. Dabrowski!"

"Please come in," Baba said in halting English.

It wasn't until the doughnut man came through the door that Ting noticed his hands were full. He extended them to Mama and handed over a big box along with a tray that had three cups sitting inside.

"Thank you for the turkey. Ting said you weren't sure what to do with all that food. I guess it must be quite different than what you're used to cooking. I'll tell you what. I'll bring some leftovers over the day after Thanksgiving for you to try, and then next year you won't be so anxious to give that bird away!" Mr. Dabrowski let out a booming laugh, then continued. "I thought you might enjoy a box of doughnuts and some hot chocolate to wash them down with."

For the second time that day Ting found herself acting as translator.

"Well, I need to get back to the shop. Drink those hot chocolates while they're still warm!"

And as Ting followed Mr. Dabrowski's instructions, she thought she had never tasted a better drink in her whole life.

· Chapter 25 ·

Ting was standing in front of the cracked mirror in the bathroom of their apartment, practising saying "trick or treat" over and over again. Hearing it come out all wrong for what seemed like the thousandth time, she stuck her tongue out at herself, then stomped her foot on the floor in exasperation.

"What are you doing, Ting Ting? Are you okay?"

"Yes, Mama. I'm fine," she replied in a mix of Chinese and English.

Ting was finding this happening more and more often. Without thinking about it, she'd find her sentences sprinkled with English words even though she meant for them all to be Chinese. Mama would give her funny looks when it happened, and Ting wasn't sure what she was thinking in those moments. But Ting had soon found out exactly what *was* going through her mother's mind.

It started out as a wonderful surprise. One week before Halloween she arrived home from school to find a letter from Yin waiting for her on the table. This was the first letter she had received from Yin, and she was so excited to see what her friend had written that she dropped her books right there in the middle of the floor and tore the letter open. Mama must have known she was excited because she didn't even scold her for being so careless.

Dear Ting,
I hope you are fine. I am well. School is very dull without you here. I walk there alone every day and think of the times we used to walk together. I am glad to have your fish to keep me company.
   We have a new teacher this year. His name is Teacher Cui. He makes history even more boring than Teacher Chen did.

When Ting looked at the next sentence she realized she didn't know what the Chinese character at the beginning said. Surprised, she looked up at her mother and said, "Mama, I can't remember this character. What is it?"

With a look of shock on her face Mama said, "'Today.' That character says 'today.' How could you forget it? You learned that character when you were first at school!"

Several more times while reading, Ting got stuck on characters but decided not to ask Mama for help. There was something about the look on her face that worried Ting. So she just kept reading until the meaning of the character became clear from what the rest of the sentence said. *Hey*, she thought, *just like I do when I am reading Little House in the Big Woods*!

Today I almost fell asleep in class. Junjie did fall asleep last week and had to do extra duties around the school. It is odd, though. I think Junjie actually misses you. He talks about you all the time and in a nice way, not like before.

I liked hearing about Canada. Please write and tell me more stories about your life there.

Your friend,

Yin

Now standing in front of the mirror practising her Halloween words, Ting thought with regret that she should never have asked Mama for help with that character. Last night she'd overheard her parents talking about the incident.

"But Shu, it is good that Ting is starting to use English words. She needs to learn quickly so she can keep up with her class at school."

"Yes, I agree she needs to learn English, and I am glad she is able to learn so much faster than we are. But I do *not* like it that she is mixing together her English and Chinese. Worse still is the fact that she is actually forgetting her Chinese characters!"

"I think it is hard for her to keep them all in her head along with the new things she is learning. We're going to have to accept that she will not be as fluent in reading Chinese as she would be if we had stayed in China."

"Well, I asked at the refugee society when I was there last week, and they told me there is such a thing as Chinese school. It is every Saturday. I think we need to sign Ting up for this school."

Oh, no! Ting had thought. One of the things she liked most about school in Canada was the fact that she didn't have to go on Saturdays. Now Mama was talking about signing her up for Chinese classes!

Sure enough, the very next Saturday Ting found herself escorted to a small, run-down building several blocks from where they lived. When they found the room at the back that was indicated on the sheet of paper Mama was carrying, the scene that met Ting's eyes did nothing to dispel the gloom she felt at having to be there.

The room had one bare light bulb hanging from the ceiling. Ting looked at its pathetic glow and thought they might as well turn it off and save the electricity. There were no desks—just three grimy-looking tables with some very uncomfortable-looking chairs scattered around them. Seven of those chairs had children seated in them, sullen looks firmly planted on each of their faces.

The teacher stood at the front of the class in a rumpled shirt and pants that ended about ten centimetres above his ankles. Mama had told her before they arrived that his name was Teacher Huan. In Chinese *Huan* meant "happiness." Ting looked at the man and thought, *Not a chance.* Mama talked to Teacher Huan for a few minutes, then smiled at Ting and left the room. She had told Ting she would be there to meet her after her class finished at noon.

The class was scheduled to start at nine o'clock. That meant three long hours of sitting there in the dismal, dark room before she could escape. She sighed and looked at Teacher Huan as he began to speak.

Oh, no, Ting thought as she heard the first words come out of his mouth.

Never before had she heard someone speak Chinese so slowly. It was as if each word was being pulled out of him against his will. She had a quick look around the classroom to see if other students were noticing this defect in their teacher. They all had glazed looks on their faces, and Ting realized that this must not be their first class with Teacher Huan.

To make matters worse, he was teaching them the most basic Chinese characters, ones Ting had first learned when she started school as a little girl. She wondered if this was because he was so slow that he was still stuck at the beginning. She was sure the other students must be frustrated by this, but when she looked around she was surprised to see them all bent over their paper, working hard at copying the three simple characters Teacher Huan had written on the board.

Finally, a five-minute break came at ten o'clock. The only thing Ting had been looking forward to about the Saturday Chinese class was being able to talk to other kids in her native language.

"*Ni hao!*" she said in greeting, approaching a girl who looked close to her own age. "Have you been coming to this class for very long?"

The girl stared at her blankly, as if she hadn't heard

a word Ting had said. She decided she would try again. Maybe the girl was just shy.

"Have you lived in Canada for very long? What part of China are you from?"

The girl continued to stare, then shrugged her shoulders and walked away. Ting stood there wondering what she had done to offend this girl. Just then she heard, or rather smelled, Teacher Huan walk up behind her. No wonder he had been so eager to excuse the class for their break. Clearly he had been in a rush to go smoke a cigarette. Ting *hated* the smell of cigarettes.

"She does not speak Chinese. She cannot understand what you are saying." He was speaking Chinese, but not much faster than he did when teaching.

Ting turned and looked at Teacher Huan in surprise. "Why is she in this class, then? Surely she is Chinese."

"Her grandparents are from China. This girl was born here, as were her parents before her. Her parents want her to learn to speak Chinese, so she is being sent to my class."

"What about the other students?" Ting asked.

"Much the same. Chinese heritage, but no language skills."

No wonder the class is so basic! thought Ting.

For the first time that day, she felt happy. Surely now Mama would agree to let her stop attending. Ting's Saturdays would be free once more!

· Chapter 26 ·

But Ting's hopes were soon dashed. She pleaded, she cried, she sulked…and she failed to convince Mama that she should be allowed to quit the Saturday Chinese class. Baba even tried to intervene on Ting's behalf, but there was no changing Mama's mind.

"Surely, Shu, it is a waste of time for Ting to sit in this beginner Chinese class on Saturday mornings."

"Not if I speak with the teacher and ask for her to be given more advanced work. I'm sure he'll agree to this request."

"You can ask, but even if he says yes it means she will at best be given only a small amount of attention. He has his other students to think about."

But there was no changing Mama's mind when it was made up. The Saturday morning drudgery would continue. Mama had made it clear there would be no more discussion.

That decision would have made it Ting's worst day in Canada if it hadn't been for the conversation she overheard much later that evening.

"You know, Shu, Ting very much wants to do this thing called Halloween."

"It sounds disgraceful, going door to door begging for candy."

"That is how it seems to us, but it must not seem that way to Canadians or they wouldn't let their children do it." There was a pause, then Baba continued. "Ting needs to feel like she belongs in this place. How can we expect her to succeed in Canada if we hold her back from doing the things other Canadians do?"

After another hesitation, one in which Ting hardly dared breathe, she heard Mama say, "Fine. She can do this begging day." Then she quickly added, "But she will also attend Chinese school."

Ting smiled, hardly hearing Mama's final comment, and fell asleep with a light heart.

The next morning when Ting woke up, the first thought she had was *I get to go trick or treating*! That thought was followed by a new, worrisome one. *What costume will I wear? I don't own anything to make a costume out of.*

She continued to think about this dilemma while she ate her breakfast and then helped wash the dishes.

"Ting Ting! You need to get busy and wipe these dishes dry. You are standing as still as one of those totem poles at Stanley Park."

That's it! Ting thought. *I can dress up as a totem pole*!

With that, Ting started drying dishes as fast as she dared without risking dropping one on the floor and breaking it. If she did that, her mother might not be so willing to help with her plan.

"Mama, can we go to the store to see if they have any old cardboard boxes?"

"Whatever for?"

"I need to have a costume for Halloween, and I know what I can make—a totem pole!"

Her mama looked at her for a minute, then nodded her head and slowly started to smile. Ting had known Mama would like the idea. She might not be happy about the fact Ting was going to go beg at people's doors, but she did want her daughter to have fun, and there had been precious little of that since she had arrived.

"That's a good idea. But the totem poles are brightly coloured. You will need to get some paints, too."

Ting could hardly believe her ears! She knew they were very short of money. She had heard her parents discussing it again just a few nights before. And now Mama was saying they could buy some paints to make her Halloween costume. She put down her dishtowel and gave her mama a big hug.

After they had gone to the laundry and put their clothes into one of the washing machines, they headed down to the store where they had purchased Ting's school supplies. They walked up and down aisles until they found the one that sold bottles of paint. Ting now understood what the numbers meant, so she knew how much each kind cost. She also had enough English skills that she was able to ask the lady working in the store what kind of paint would work best on cardboard. When the lady heard the reason Ting needed the paint, not only did she help her choose the right kind, but she also asked if she needed some cardboard for her project.

"Yes, please!"

So the two of them walked back home, Mama with one huge flattened cardboard box in her hands and Ting with another. When they got back to the apartment, they sat on the floor, the cardboard, paints, a roll of tape, and a pair of scissors spread out before them. For two solid hours they worked together, talking about which animal figures they should cut out, what colours they would paint each one, and how they would tape the horizontal crosspiece to the main vertical piece without the whole thing falling apart. Baba, with his engineering skills, got involved at that point and joined them on the floor, finding a way to attach the pieces so that you could not even see the tape.

It was a fun-filled day, and at the end of it Ting was covered in paint from head to toe. She looked almost as colourful as the totem pole itself. Even her hair had some bright yellow paint in it. When she looked in the mirror that night she was surprised to see it there.

"Hey! I look like Hannah!" Ting remembered how surprised she had been by her friend's pale hair when she had first met her. *The girl with no hair colour*, she thought. Then Ting looked in the mirror and tried again to say those magic but oh-so-difficult words. "Trick or treat."

She could not believe it. It had sounded right. She said them again just to be sure. Yes, she really could say it and sound like a Canadian! Unlike last time, when she had looked at the girl in the mirror and stuck her tongue out at her, this time she gave that girl a huge smile.

· Chapter 27 ·

The day after Halloween, Ting looked out the window and sighed. *Does it do nothing but rain here in Vancouver?* she asked herself. She decided it was time to write another letter to Yin.

Dear Yin,

I was so happy to receive your letter! I am sorry you have to walk to school by yourself. Hopefully you will find a friend to walk with soon. I am also sorry Teacher Cui is no better at teaching history than Teacher Chen. I think the reason Junjie misses me is that he no longer has anyone to torment.

Yesterday there was an exciting holiday here in Canada. Well, it isn't really a holiday, but it sure seemed like one! It is called Halloween. Kids dress up in costumes and go knock on the doors of homes in their neighbourhood. When the door is opened you call out in a loud voice, "Trick or treat!" You hold out the bag you are carrying, and the person living there places candy or other treats in it. I never could have imagined such a wonderful holiday before I came to Canada!

Remember that brown milk I told you about? It turns

out that they have two different kinds of brown milk here.
The one I mentioned earlier is cold, but I now know there
is also a brown milk that is hot. I have tasted it and it is
the best thing I have ever had to drink. The man that sells
doughnuts gave it to me. Oh——doughnuts are what you
call the baked treats with holes in them I told you about
in my last letter. I have had those now, too, and they are
delicious. I think I like them even better than stick candy.

Your friend,

Ting

Ting couldn't stop thinking about last night. She looked over at her collection of candy, piled high in one of her mama's bowls. She didn't know there could be so many different kinds of candy! There were wrappers of all different sizes, shapes, and colours. She had already eaten several when she got home last night, but then Mama said she had better save the rest for later or she would get a tummy ache.

Ting was surprised Mama hadn't said her teeth might rot out like Yeye's. She wondered if that was because it made Mama sad to think about their family back in China the same way it made Ting feel sad inside. She missed her yimas so much and worried that Yeye would grow old and die before she could return to China to visit him. It was easier not to mention them.

Her sad thoughts didn't last long, however. There were too many happy thoughts about Halloween to take their place. She had felt so proud each time a door opened and she was able to say those difficult words perfectly! Many people guessed right away that she was dressed up as a totem pole, which had also pleased her.

There were so many other children out that night, also going door to door, that when they got home Mama said she thought maybe this Halloween thing might be okay after all. Ting smiled when she remembered catching Mama taking one of the candies out of the big bowl when she thought Ting wasn't looking. *I think she has a sweet tooth just like me!*

Then there had been the fireworks. Better even than the candy and the costume, partly because they were such a surprise and partly because they reminded Ting so much of her life back in China. Hannah hadn't told her there would be fireworks at Halloween. In fact, Ting hadn't known Canadians even had fireworks.

When she saw the first bottle rocket go high into the air, making the telltale sound as it did so, she had pointed and said to her father, "Baba! Look!" All through the night people continued to decorate the sky with colourful, noisy displays, which made Ting feel happy and homesick all at once.

The fireworks must have reminded Baba of their home back in China, too. When Ting had pointed out that first one exploding in the night sky, he had immediately launched into yet another of his Chinese history lessons.

"Ting Ting, did you know that the Chinese were

responsible for inventing fireworks? It was during the Song Dynasty that they first made an appearance."

Of course Ting knew this. There wasn't a Chinese person anywhere who did not know that they were the ones responsible for inventing fireworks. It was not the first time that he had pointed out the Chinese origins of something in Canada, either. Once, when they were walking through the small park near their apartment, he had pointed into the sky and said, "Ting Ting, see that kite? Did you know the Chinese were the first to make kites?" Another time, as they passed one of the many little restaurants along their street, Baba had pointed at the menu in the window and said, "We were the first to make menus. Did you know that, Ting Ting?" And just last night before bed, when Mama told her to brush her teeth extra carefully, Baba had immediately added, "You know, Ting Ting, the Chinese invented the toothbrush during the Ming Dynasty."

Ting thought Baba was starting to sound a lot like Teacher Chen with his talk of dynasties. But what surprised her was the fact that she was finding all of this interesting. Even the mention of the dreaded word *dynasty* no longer triggered a yawn the way it used to during her history class in Jinan.

Perhaps, thought Ting, *I now understand why it is important to remember such things*. And as she looked out the window again, she could see the clouds separating and her mountains starting to peek through in the distance.

· Chapter 28 ·

A week after Halloween, Hannah handed Ting a card tucked inside a bright green envelope. "It's an invitation to my birthday party," she told Ting. "Do you think you can come?"

Ting thought about it for a minute. Her mama would be nervous about letting Ting go into a stranger's home. Hannah wasn't really a stranger, though, only the rest of her family.

"I not sure," Ting said hesitantly, searching for the right English words. She could see Hannah's face fall, so she quickly added, "Do not worry, I talk to my mom."

Although Ting had told Hannah not to worry, she herself was worried. This was the first time Ting had been invited to a Canadian home. Complicating the situation was the fact it was for a birthday party. She knew Mama would worry about what was expected for such an event.

That afternoon she went straight home from school. She didn't linger on the school grounds to visit with Hannah until Mrs. Larsson came, nor did she stop to look in the window of the doughnut shop. She went running up the stairs and burst through their apartment door, holding the invitation out as she did so.

"Look, Mama! It's an invitation to Hannah's birthday party. Remember, Hannah is the girl from school I have told you about, the one who has been so kind to me? The party is next Saturday at two o'clock. It's going to be at Hannah's house. The address is right here on the card. See? Here, inside."

Out of breath after that outburst, Ting looked up at her mama expectantly. She could see Mama's forehead wrinkle in that way that meant she was thinking.

"Can I go, Mama? Please can I go?"

Then, in what came as a total surprise for Ting, her mama said, "Yes, I think it would be very nice for you to go to this girl's party. We will have to figure out ahead of time how to take the bus to this address so you do not arrive late."

Ting could not believe her ears! Never in a thousand years would she have thought her mama would say yes so readily. She couldn't wait to go to school the next day and tell Hannah the good news. She would also have to quiz Hannah closely about what a birthday party was like here in Canada so she would know just what was expected of her. Ting's birthdays in China had been spent with family. She had no idea what would happen at a party that included friends.

• • •

"Well," Hannah said the next day during recess, "usually there is a cake, one with fancy decorations on it,

145

and sometimes the cake is even made of ice cream. Sometimes there is a movie to watch, or some kind of activity or game that everyone plays. And there are presents, of course!"

Ting thought it all sounded wonderful—right up to the part about the presents. What on earth would she get Hannah for a present, and how on earth would she pay for it? She didn't want her friend to see that she was concerned, so she simply said it sounded like a lot of fun. And it would be, if Ting could find a way to get her friend a present.

That evening over dinner, Ting brought up the problem of the present.

"I asked Hannah today what a birthday is like here in Canada. She said that everyone brings presents, but I have nothing to give."

"What kinds of things do people give as presents?" Mama asked.

Ting realized she hadn't asked Hannah that question. She had been so worried when she heard that presents were expected that she hadn't thought to ask anything more.

"I don't know, Mama."

Mama sat with her thinking look on her face for some time before saying, "I have an idea! When you get home from school tomorrow, we will take the bus to the thrift store and see if they have any nice wool and some knitting needles. I've seen such things before at the back of the store, sitting in baskets on the floor."

Ting thought about this idea. Mama was a very good knitter. It got very cold in Jinan in the winter, and Mama had knit many hats, mittens, and scarves for Ting to wear so she could stay warm. She had even knit her several sweaters, including a blue one with a bright red kitten on the front. Ting had been sad to leave that sweater behind, but it was almost too small, and there had been no room in her bag for it anyway. Then Ting thought about how long it had taken her mama to knit that sweater.

"Do you have time to knit something for Hannah? The party is in just four more days."

"That is enough time to knit a pair of mittens, and maybe even a hat."

As promised, the next day Mama took Ting to the thrift store to find some yarn. The people at the refugee society had told Ting's parents about the thrift store, explaining it was a place to buy inexpensive second-hand items. Several times they had gone, and the last time they'd been able to find a backpack for Ting for school. Ting had been very happy about that, even if the backpack was missing a strap and had a small ink stain on the front. It meant that now she could hide her ugly brown paper lunch bag inside so the other kids couldn't see it. Even more important than its ability to hide her lunch bag was its power to make her feel more like everyone else. It made her feel like she belonged.

They both hunched over the baskets, digging through the meagre offerings of yarn.

"What about this one?" Mama asked, holding up a ball that was an awful shade of pink.

"Ugh!"

Mama held up several more possibilities, all of which Ting immediately rejected. Finally, just when Ting was despairing of ever finding something her friend would like, she reached down and her hands touched something very soft. She pulled it out and looked at the bright blue yarn in her hands. It was the same colour as the sky on the days Ting could see her mountains.

"This one, Mama!"

Mama's eyes lit up when she took the blue wool from Ting's hands and held it in her own. She felt the yarn, then rubbed it against her cheek and smiled.

"You have done very well, Ting Ting! This is not just any old yarn. It is cashmere. Cashmere yarn is very valuable. This will make a lovely pair of mittens for your friend."

After finding some knitting needles, they paid for their purchases and then hurried home so Mama could start knitting. For the rest of that week, every time Ting saw her mama she was busily working away with the needles in her hands. She even knit while she had the notes from her English night class spread out in front of her! By Friday night the mittens were finished. Ting had a present for the party the next day.

• • •

Saturday morning crawled along. First there was the endless Chinese class, and then, at home, Ting kept looking at the small clock in their kitchen. It seemed as if the hands were never getting any closer to one-thirty, the time they needed to leave for the bus if Ting was to arrive at the party in time. Her gift was safely tucked away in her backpack, wrapped and ready to give to Hannah.

The wrapping had also posed a dilemma for Ting. They had no wrapping paper at home, and Ting did not want to ask her parents to spend money on such a thing when there were so many other things they *really* needed. She worried about what to do for some time, and then an idea popped into her head. She had saved the beautiful red embroidered cloth and green silk ribbon Mei Yima had wrapped her writing paper in. It would be perfect for wrapping Hannah's gift!

Delighted, she thought, *That will mean the whole present is Chinese, even the wrapping.*

When Baba had seen the cashmere yarn, he'd proceeded to tell Ting how almost all the world's cashmere came from China, and how, no doubt, this very ball of yarn had originated in their home country. And, of course, Ting knew that the silk in the cloth and ribbon were Chinese. Even the person who'd knit the mittens was Chinese!

Finally the time came for Ting and Mama to catch their bus. When they reached the right stop, they walked to the address on the card and stopped in amazement in front of a huge house. It was big enough for many families! They looked at the number on the card again, and it definitely matched the one on the huge home in front of them.

Ting suddenly had butterflies in her stomach. They opened the gate and walked up the brick path, lined on both sides with beautiful plants. When they got to the front door, Mama knocked on the heavy wood, at first softly, then harder. She was still knocking when the door suddenly swung open.

"Yes, may I help you?"

A lady who looked like an older version of Hannah was standing there looking out at them. She even had the same colour hair as Hannah, which Ting now knew was called blond. There was the sound of running feet, and Hannah appeared in the doorway next to her mom.

"Mom, this is Ting!"

The look on her mother's face instantly changed from one of confusion to one of welcome.

"Oh, hello! Come on in. Hannah has told me all about you. I guess I was confused by the knocking—I was expecting to hear the doorbell."

Ting had no idea what a "doorbell" was, but she was relieved to know she was at the right house, and to see that Hannah's mom looked every bit as friendly as her daughter. Hannah was grabbing Ting's hand, trying to pull her away from the door.

"Come on, everyone is up in my room. We're all painting each other's fingernails."

Ting turned to her mama and said goodbye, then hurried to keep up with Hannah, who was taking the stairs two at a time.

What followed was both wonderful and horrible. Hannah's friends were all very kind to Ting. Well, all except for one girl with red hair who rolled her eyes and sighed impatiently every time Ting said anything. Ting knew she spoke slower than everyone else and didn't need this girl to remind her. She also knew that she was a guest in this home, and therefore she dared not confront the girl about her rudeness. Instead, she chose to ignore her. At first it was difficult, but as the afternoon wore on, Ting found she hardly noticed the red-haired girl anymore.

They painted each other's nails. Ting's were a bright purple, and every time she looked at her hands they made her smile. Then they watched a video called *The Jungle Book*. Ting got so caught up in the story that she even forgot about her purple fingernails until it was finished.

After the movie Hannah's mom called them downstairs, saying it was time for cake and presents. Ting couldn't wait for her friend to open the gift she had for her! They all sat around in a circle on the floor, each one handing Hannah a gift, which she opened before the next person handed her a gift. Ting watched with a growing sense of horror as Hannah opened lovely, expensive presents.

There was a new jacket, a fancy box filled with a dozen different colours of nail polish, a game called Sorry, a book called *Anne of Green Gables*—that had been from the annoying girl with the red hair—and then a present in the fanciest wrapping of all. Hannah gasped and oohed and aahed when she saw what it was. Ting gasped, too, but for completely different reasons, as she saw her friend pull out of the wrapping a beautiful pink scarf, hat, and mittens. They were fluffy, and the hat and mittens had beads that sparkled, beads that were sewn in a snowflake pattern.

Hannah thanked the girl who had given her the lovely set, then turned expectantly to Ting. Ting knew she could not pull Hannah's gift out of her backpack, not now. The humiliation would be more than she could bear. Thinking quickly, she lied, "I forgot your present at my home. Sorry."

Ting lowered her eyes, not wanting to see the disappointment on her friend's face, and not wanting her friend to see the embarrassment on her own.

· Chapter 29 ·

During the bus ride home, and after she got back to the apartment, Ting didn't say a word. She just sat in the chair by the window with her library book in her hands. She wasn't really reading it, just holding it and staring out at the mountains.

She could feel her parents watching her, but they didn't question her until dinnertime. Then Baba said, "You're very quiet, Ting Ting. Did you have a good time at Hannah's party?"

In words that could barely be heard Ting answered, "I suppose."

Baba pressed on. "What kinds of things did you do?"

"Well, when I first got there we painted each other's fingernails." She held up her hands for her parents to see. "Then we watched a movie about a bear and a boy. It was good, even though it was sometimes hard to understand what they were saying. The best parts were the songs." They all had a good laugh as Ting sang a few lines from "The Bare Necessities."

At this point Ting stopped. How could she explain about the rest of the party? She just couldn't tell Mama about the mittens. It would hurt her mama's feelings to know Ting was too ashamed of the gift that Mama had made to give it to her friend. As Ting sat there, trying to think of a way to explain her humiliation, she could feel a tear making its way down her cheek. Then she felt Mama's soft hand reach out and cup her chin.

"Ting Ting, whatever is wrong? Were they unkind to you at the party?"

Ting looked up and saw the love and concern on her mama's face, and that was all it took. She burst into tears, and all the misery from the party came pouring out. Finally, she came to the part about the cake.

"It was horrible! When we went to eat the birthday cake, Hannah's mom put a piece on each person's plate, along with a fork to eat it with. I have never used a fork before," she sobbed.

"Shh, take a breath." Ting felt herself being wrapped in her mama's warm arms.

"All the other girls were talking and laughing as they started to eat their cake. I...I..."

Ting got stuck there, sobs taking over again as she thought of what had happened next.

"I watched carefully to see what the others were doing. It looked easy enough. But when I held my fork, this nasty girl with red hair pointed at me and said, 'Look, she holds her fork like a baby!' A few of the other girls giggled when they looked at me. Then, as I went to take my first bite, something happened." This brought on a fresh wave of tears. Mama continued to stroke Ting's hair, waiting for her to be able to talk again.

"I don't know what happened. I was probably holding

the fork all wrong. One minute the cake was in front of me and the next it was...it was...on the floor."

Ting had barely been able to choke the last words out, but she wasn't finished. The thoughts that had been swirling around in her head while she stared out the window, the thoughts she couldn't escape, came spilling out in a rush.

"I don't fit in here. I can't speak English as well as the other kids. I wear old clothes that come out of bags from the refugee society or from the thrift store. I take my lunch to school every day in an old paper bag. I don't even eat right. Nobody here uses chopsticks. I want to go home. I want to go back to China!"

It was at that point that Baba spoke up.

"I'm sorry the party did not go well for you, Ting Ting. I am also sorry that you feel you do not fit in here in your new home. I have to admit I often feel the same way."

Ting looked up at Baba in surprise when he said this. Then she thought about how he did not have a job because his English wasn't good enough, and about how Canada wouldn't recognize his credentials.

"You too, Baba?"

"Yes, me too. But then I remember that we have only been here a short while. We will learn. You, Mama, and me. We will all learn how to be more Canadian. But that does not mean I ever want you to forget that you are *also* Chinese. It is a heritage you should be proud of."

Ting's crying began to slow as Baba continued.

"Did you know the Chinese actually invented the fork?"

She looked at him in surprise.

"Forks were used during the Shang Dynasty but have been discovered in burial sites from even earlier times. Their use was abandoned when it became clear that chopsticks are superior in every way."

Eyes twinkling, Baba added, "But, since we live here where they are still eating like those of the Shang Dynasty, perhaps we could buy a few of these forks and you could practise with them here at home."

Ting wiped her tears away and went over to give him a hug.

"Thank you, Baba."

"And now I suggest, since it is Saturday night and we all need to practise fitting into our new country, that we turn on our little television set and watch *Hockey Night in Canada*."

• • •

At lunchtime on Monday Ting surprised Hannah by pulling something other than her paper bag out of her backpack.

"Here," she said, handing Hannah her belated birthday present.

Then she watched nervously as Hannah took the package and began unwrapping it.

"This is beautiful! Did you wrap it yourself?"

"Yes, this is how gifts are wrapped in China. Wrapping is very important."

Hannah slowly untied the green ribbon that

surrounded the bright red cloth. Ting held her breath as Hannah pulled back the edges of the cloth to reveal the mittens Mama had worked so hard on. She grew alarmed as she saw the look on Hannah's face. Her friend was not smiling. Instead, she wore a serious expression as she looked over at Ting.

"Did you make these?"

Ting's face burned with shame. Now she would have to admit to her friend that her gift had not come from a store the way the other girls' gifts had. That, in fact, the gift had been made by her mama.

Ting's voice could barely be heard as she said, "My mom knit them for you."

"Oh, Ting! They are beautiful!" Hannah said, her voice full of emotion. "They remind me so much of my grandma. She knit me mittens every winter, but now that she is gone I thought I would have to go through this winter without any hand-knit mittens. Every time I wear them I will think of her"—she hugged Ting—"and my best friend."

Once Ting recovered from the shock she said, "But you have the nice pink ones from the party."

Now Hannah's voice got very quiet.

"I wouldn't want Brittany to know, but I hate the colour pink. Plus my grandma always used to say there was nothing like a pair of hand-knit mittens to keep your hands toasty warm on a cold winter's day. She was right—the store-bought ones let the wind and cold go right through them. Please tell your mother how much I like them and that I said thanks."

157

That night, when Ting went to give her mama a goodnight hug, she said, "Hannah loved the mittens you made for her, Mama. She said to tell you thank you. She said they reminded her of her grandma who used to knit her a pair every winter."

As Ting pulled the covers up, she thought about the other thing Hannah had said. The thing that was even better than her liking the mittens. Hannah had called Ting her best friend.

· Chapter 30 ·

All through November, Ting wondered whether or not Mr. Long would decide she was ready to graduate from the ESL class. Ting longed to be done with it, but not because she didn't like Mr. Long. He was very kind and had spent extra time with Ting. She especially liked it when he helped her with *Little House in the Big Woods*.

In spite of her success reading the first sentence that day in the library, Ting had found the book challenging. Sometimes she could figure out only a word or two in the evenings when she was studying. But even on the days she made little progress, Ting still loved looking at the book. There were wonderful pictures of Laura and Mary in the Big Woods. Ting would try to imagine what it would have been like to be a little girl who lived so long ago, in a place so different from any she had ever known.

What would it be like to live where there was nothing but trees and wild animals for miles and miles and miles? Even though Vancouver seemed empty compared to her home in Jinan, it still had many people. Ting could not imagine a place with nobody but their little family.

And the thought of all those wild animals sent a chill running down Ting's spine. Imagine lying in bed at night listening to the wolves howl and prowl around your house! Although she rarely needed her beloved blanket anymore, whenever Ting thought about those wolves her hand would reach down to grab it, then wrap it protectively around her neck.

But the thing Ting marvelled at the most when she read about Laura had nothing to do with the log house, or the Big Woods, or any of the wild animals the Ingalls family shared those woods with. It was the fact that Laura had two sisters. *What would it be like to have even one sister?* she wondered.

Growing up in China, Ting hadn't known a single child who had a brother or sister. The government made people pay heavy fines if they had more than one child, so hardly anyone did. Ting had noticed right away when she got to Canada that the government here didn't seem to care how many children a family had. It must have been that way where Laura lived, too.

On the last day of the month, when it was time to go down the hall to the ESL class, Ting had a difficult time not running. She walked as fast as she thought she could get away with and pushed the door open before any of the other students were even close. Then she stopped in surprise.

The room had colourful paper streamers hanging

from the ceiling, along with some balloons. Mr. Long stood at the front of the room next to a flat cake—the biggest cake Ting had ever seen! He smiled at her and told her to come on in and have a look. When Ting went forward to see the cake, she was even more surprised. Written in big red letters were these words:

Well Done, Ting!

"It is your last day to be in our class, Ting. This deserves a celebration."

Ting could tell the other students were a bit envious of the fact that she was able to stop attending the class and they weren't, but the cake helped ease any hard feelings. Of course, Mr. Long turned the whole celebration into a language lesson, pointing out the words for everything they were doing. Ting was especially glad Mama had found some forks at the thrift store. She had been practising with them for over a week and now felt quite confident picking one up and eating her piece of cake with it.

When the bell rang dismissing them from the ESL class, Mr. Long asked Ting to stay behind a few minutes.

"Ting, I wanted to let you know that you have broken a school record. You have graduated from the ESL class here faster than any student before you. I am very proud of your accomplishment. Also, I have a small gift for you."

Mr. Long then reached into his desk, pulled out a small rectangular package, and handed it to Ting.

"Thank you," she said. Then she just stood there, not quite sure what to do next.

"Well, aren't you going to open it?"

"Oh. Yes!"

Ting carefully removed the paper, intending to keep it, and stared in amazement. It was a book—but not just any book. It was a copy of *Little House in the Big Woods*. She could not believe it! She had already renewed her library copy twice, and the librarian had explained to her that she could not renew it again. Ting had been worried about this, as she could read only a little bit at a time and knew she would never be able to finish the book before it had to be returned. Now she had her very own copy, one that she could keep forever.

"Thank you, Mr. Long!" It was hard to tell who had the bigger smile—Ting or Mr. Long.

• • •

From that moment on, Ting really felt like a part of her regular class at school. Being pulled out for the ESL class had made her feel like an outsider. Now she was just like all the other kids in her class. She felt as though she belonged.

The classes she had been missing while she attended the ESL class were English and social studies. Ting was confused by the name "social studies" and was somewhat dismayed to find out it included history. The yawns she'd stifled during Teacher Chen's boring lectures immediately popped into her mind.

As it turned out, Ting quickly discovered she

enjoyed Canadian history. She loved hearing about the people who explored and settled new territory. Mrs. McBride read them a story about an explorer named David Thompson. Ting thought about all the distance he had travelled and how lonely he must have felt. Another time she read a book called *Madeleine Takes Command*, about a fourteen-year-old girl who defends the fort where she lives from attacking Mohawks.

Even better than learning about explorers and settlers, however, was hearing about the native people. Ting listened, fascinated, to stories about how they carved canoes out of trees, made homes out of animal hides, hunted buffalo, and used stories to explain the world around them. She thought about how the Chinese did the same thing with stories and was happy to feel this connection with the First Peoples of her new country. Ting also learned that there were many different groups of native people, and each group used the particular resources around them in very smart ways to survive.

Before these lessons, Ting had thought *all* native people carved totem poles. Now she knew that it was just the people who lived along the coast—where she lived, she thought proudly. She also learned that it was only the Inuit who lived in igloos, not other Canadians, and that nowadays the Inuit had houses similar to the ones other Canadians lived in. She felt a little embarrassed when she thought back to the time her parents were living here without her and she had wondered if they were staying in an igloo.

The English class was very challenging for Ting. Her reading skills were still not up to the same level as the other students', but she was making rapid progress. Writing was even more difficult, and the teacher sent Ting home with extra work each day.

Ting didn't really mind. Overall she found school here in Canada to be much easier than in China. So much time in China was spent learning characters. Every night there had been characters to study. And the school days were much shorter in Canada, so even when she added on the extra homework she had been given, it still didn't make for as long a school day as she'd had back in Jinan.

One wonderful surprise in her English class had been when she found out that every day Mrs. McBride read aloud to them. On Ting's first day in the class they were just starting a book called *A Little Princess*. Ting couldn't wait to hear the next part, and she would sigh heavily when the teacher closed the book each day and said they would read more tomorrow. She thought about how lonely Sara, the girl in the story, must have felt at the boarding school, and then when they said her father was dead she really *was* alone. Ting was glad that even when she was separated from her parents she'd had her yimas to take care of her. It had been lonely, but she had never been alone.

After they finished *A Little Princess*, Mrs. McBride said they would start a new book on the following Monday. Ting wondered all that weekend what the new story would be about. She didn't think it could ever be as good as the one they had just finished. It turned out she was wrong.

On Monday morning at read-aloud time, Mrs. McBride said their new book was the first in a series, and it was written by a Canadian author. She hoped everyone would like it enough that they would want to read the rest of the books on their own. Ting looked on expectantly as her teacher held up the new book, and then she let out a gasp. It was the same one that Hannah had been given on her birthday!

Ting still felt anger rise up in her when she thought about the red-haired girl who had given that present to Hannah, and how she had made fun of Ting over the way she held the fork. Hannah had later told her that the girl's name was Alice. Alice was Hannah's cousin, and Hannah's mom had made her invite Alice to the party. She told Ting not to worry about what Alice had done and said that she was annoying and always had been. Ting had then told Hannah about her cousin Junjie. They'd both laughed extra hard about how Junjie had been made to do all of Ting's cleaning jobs for the rest of the school year.

Ting just knew she wasn't going to like this book. She was convinced of that—right up until Mrs. McBride opened the book and started reading.

· Chapter 31 ·

Dear Yin,

There is so much to tell you. I don't know if this paper will be able to hold all of my news! Oh—I hope you are well. I meant to say that right away, but I was so excited to tell you what has been happening that I forgot.

First of all, I have been to a birthday party. It was for my new friend Hannah. Did I tell you about Hannah? She has hair that at first seems to be without colour, but when you look at it closely it is a very light yellow colour. Canadians call it blond. Anyway, at her party we painted our fingernails bright colours. Then we watched a movie about a boy who talks to a bear.

Next Hannah opened her gifts. She got such expensive items! Mama knit her some mittens out of some pretty blue yarn we found. Remember how good a knitter Mama is?

Then they did the strangest thing. There was a large cake and it had nine candles on top of it—the same number as Hannah's age. They were all burning and Hannah had to make a wish, then blow the candles out. She got them all out with one breath, so she will get her wish. I don't know what she wished for. The wish has to be kept a secret.

Ting stopped here and thought about whether to tell Yin about the bad things that had happened that day. She decided it might make Yin feel sad to know that she had been laughed at.

The party was the first time I tried eating with a fork. Mama bought some and I have been practising. It is very different from using chopsticks.

I don't have to go to the special class to learn English anymore. My English still isn't good, but the teacher said I was doing well enough to be in the regular class. I am very happy about that. Mrs. McBride—that is the name of our teacher—reads to us each day. Right now she is reading a story about a girl named Anne. You can't believe all the trouble this Anne character gets into. And guess what? Anne has red hair! That is something else that takes some getting used to in Canada, all these different colours of hair.

By the time this letter reaches you, your family will be starting to plan for the New Year's Festival. Here all the talk is about Christmas. Write soon!

Your friend,

Ting

Ting sealed the letter in an envelope and placed it on the kitchen counter. Mama said she would mail it for her the next time she went to the post office. Ting was glad it didn't cost very much to mail a letter. They were still short of money, and Baba hadn't found a job yet. Mama was making very slow progress in her English night school, so she wasn't ready to look for a job.

Ting knew her parents were worried about their situation because she had heard them talk about it many times when they thought she was asleep. Now there was this holiday called Christmas coming up. Hannah explained to Ting that the custom was to have a big meal, usually with relatives. You also exchanged gifts with your family and friends. She said people put colourful lights outside their homes. Ting tried to picture what some of the houses on the way to school would look like with lights strung across them. It was hard to imagine.

Then Hannah told her something so strange, she wasn't sure whether to believe her.

"My favourite part of Christmas is the tree."

"The tree? What tree?"

"You buy a tree that has been cut down and put it in your house. You put a string of lights around it and then hang decorations on the branches. It makes the whole house smell yummy, and at night I like to turn out all the other lights and just sit in front of the tree dreaming about what's in the packages underneath."

Ting wasn't sure how she felt about all this. They did not have any relatives to share a meal with. They did not have any money to buy gifts. They did not have a house to hang coloured lights on. And she was fairly certain her parents would not bring a tree inside their apartment. That part was just too strange.

Ten days before Christmas was Ting's own birthday. She would be nine, just like Hannah. There wasn't enough money to have a party like her friend's, and even if they did have the money, Ting didn't really have enough friends to invite to make a real party.

In the end it was decided that Ting could invite Hannah over after school on the day before her birthday, since her actual birthday was on a Saturday and Hannah had figure skating lessons that day. Ting thought it would make the man at the airport happy to see she was celebrating on the day her papers said was her birthday, even if it wasn't the proper day!

When the Friday finally arrived, Ting suddenly felt shy about having Hannah to her apartment. Hannah's house was beautiful and filled with many lovely things. Ting remembered all the interesting pictures on the walls and the huge kitchen with so many different kinds of machines sitting on the counter, all shiny and looking as if they hardly ever got used. What would Hannah think of their small, dingy apartment with its peeling paint, second-hand furnishings, and tiny cooking area?

When the final school bell rang, releasing them for both the day and the weekend, Ting felt like slipping away before Hannah saw her. Of course, she could do no such thing. Instead she walked over to Hannah's desk and waited for her to gather her things. When Hannah saw Ting, she gave her a big smile.

"Happy birthday!"

Confused, Ting said, "You already said happy birthday this morning."

"I know, but your birthday only comes once a year, so we might as well make the most of it!"

As they walked out of the classroom and headed toward Ting's home, she couldn't help wishing she felt as excited about the day as her friend did. After all, it was *her* birthday.

By the time they arrived at the entrance to the building, Ting was so busy talking to Hannah that she forgot to be nervous. Before they went inside, they took a minute to peek inside the window of the doughnut shop. Ting felt disappointed when Mr. Dabrowski seemed not to notice her. She had secretly wished there would be a birthday doughnut for her to share with Hannah.

Ting turned away from the window and led Hannah into their building. She could see her look around at the ugly walls, but Hannah did not make any comments. She didn't even wrinkle her nose at the bad smells. *She's doing a lot better than I did the first time I came in here*, Ting thought.

"Come on, this way," she directed.

When they got to the door, it opened wide before Ting even placed her hand on the doorknob.

"Happy birthday!" called out her parents in Chinese—and then in English! Ting grinned. Mama must have asked at her night class how to say it.

Ting looked inside and could not believe her eyes! There were balloons hanging from the ceiling, and on the table was a plate stacked high with doughnuts. No wonder Mr. Dabrowski hadn't brought her a doughnut when she looked in his window. Each of the doughnuts was different. Some had frosting, some had sugar crystals, some had sprinkles the colours of the rainbow. Some were round, some were twisted around themselves, and some were the small holes from the middle of the doughnuts. There was even a present sitting on the table next to the doughnuts. Ting could tell by the way it was wrapped in a pretty cloth that it was from Mama.

Once Ting had introduced Hannah to Baba, the two girls sat on the old couch. Hannah asked Ting questions about what it had been like to grow up in China. Ting barely had time to answer one question before another one would pop out of Hannah's mouth.

"Wait, Hannah. I have something to show you."

Ting went over to the old dresser and lovingly pulled out the precious family photo album Yeye had given to her that last time she saw him. She wondered what Hannah would think of it. The cover was torn and faded, and many of the pictures were black and white, and not good quality. Hannah's mom had set out nine albums for the girls to look through at Hannah's party. Each one depicted a year of Hannah's life. Many of the pictures were cut out in cute shapes, and there were decorations glued to each of the pages and words in fancy writing accompanying them.

"Here, look at this. My grandfather gave it to me just before I moved to Canada."

The girls spent the next hour and a half looking over the pictures. Hannah sat, mesmerized, as she listened to story after story come pouring out of her friend.

These were the stories Ting had been told by Yeye, the ones he knew she would keep in her heart.

The last page of the album had just two pictures on it. One was of Ting at the park with Yeye. It had been taken the summer before she left. The other was a picture of Baba and Yeye together.

"This picture was before my dad came here to study."

"I didn't know your dad was a student," said Hannah.

"Some bad things happened in China, so my parents decided to stay in Canada. My dad had to stop going to school."

"What does your dad do now?" Hannah asked.

"He is learning English so he can get a job. He was an engineer in China. My mom is learning English, too. She was a doctor."

Just then Mama called over to Ting to tell her their meal was ready. Ting and Hannah had been so absorbed in the photo album, they had barely noticed the wonderful smells filling the apartment.

When Ting sat down at the table, she was delighted to see there were pork dumplings, bean sprouts and broccoli, rice with little bits of chicken, and cabbage and noodles in a special sauce that Ting loved. Best of all, there were no carrots or apples!

Mama had thoughtfully placed a fork at Hannah's place at the table, along with a pair of chopsticks. Ting was surprised when she saw Hannah pick up her chopsticks instead of her fork.

"I figure you had to eat cake at my house with a fork,

so it's only fair for me to use chopsticks at your house."

They all laughed, Hannah most of all, as she continued to eat her meal with the chopsticks. Ting's parents offered words of encouragement, some in Chinese and some in English. Ting showed Hannah how to hold them properly, and when the food fell off them and onto the table, Ting expertly scooped it back onto Hannah's plate for her.

"I think you were much better with your first try with a fork than I am with chopsticks!"

"But you haven't spilled food all over the floor like I did," Ting laughed.

The words were no more than out of her mouth when Hannah did just that. A whole dumpling slipped from between her chopsticks. The girls giggled again, and Baba pretended to be surprised when he looked down and saw the dumpling on his foot.

After the dinner was finished and they had helped Mama with the dishes, it was time for Ting to open her present. She carefully untied the ribbon, then slid the cloth off the present. Inside was a pair of mittens, soft and blue, just like Hannah's.

"Thank you, Mama," she said, giving her a hug.

Hannah jumped up from the table and ran to her coat, which was draped over the back of the couch. She reached into one of the pockets and pulled out the matching mittens. Then she slipped them on and came to sit by Ting.

At that moment there was a knock on the door. It was Hannah's mom.

"You can't leave until we have doughnuts!" Ting said to Hannah as Baba opened the door.

"And you need to open your present from me," Hannah said. She turned and took the big package her mom was holding.

There was an awkward moment at the door when Baba attempted to invite Hannah's mom into their apartment but couldn't come up with the right English words. Ting could see he needed rescuing, so she spoke up and asked her to please come in.

There was another awkward moment as they all stood there looking at each other. Then Mama pulled out a chair, and Ting was proud when she heard her say in almost perfect English, "Hello. Please sit."

Then Mama went into the kitchen, and while she prepared tea Hannah handed her present to Ting.

"Here—I hope you like it. My mom and I picked it out together. I'm sorry I wasn't able to give it to you earlier, but it was too big to take to school."

Ting's eyes lit up as she took the present from Hannah. It was large and quite heavy. Ting carefully tore the paper away to reveal a large cardboard box.

"Open the box, Ting!"

When Ting did so, she could hardly believe what she saw. There, gleaming up at her from inside the box, was a shiny new pair of figure skates. The white leather was the colour of snow, and the silver blades glimmered when Ting picked the skates up to admire them. She was so overwhelmed she could hardly speak.

"Th-th-thank you, Hannah. They are beautiful!"

"If they don't fit, we can exchange them. Here, let me help you try one on. Be careful of the floor. You can step on the box when you try it on."

Ting's foot slid into the skate, and then Hannah was lacing it up for her.

"The laces are so long!"

Hannah laughed. "Yes, I think I spend half my time at the skating rink dealing with the laces. But I'll help you learn how to tie them so they get tightened properly. How do they feel?"

Ting thought they fit as though they had been made just for her.

"They are perfect!"

"If you don't like the style, you can trade them for something you like better."

Ting slipped off the skate and hugged her friend.

"I would never trade them. They are wonderful. Thank you, Hannah, and thank you, Mrs. Larsson."

"Oh—and there is another part to your present. If it's okay with your parents, we would like to take you to public skating every Sunday for the next six weeks. That way I can teach you how to use them."

Ting looked at her parents to see if they approved. However, she could see by the looks on their faces that they had not been able to follow the conversation. She quickly translated and waited for their answer. When they both nodded their heads, Ting let out a squeal of delight. Then Mama said something else before Ting turned back to her friend.

"They say it is okay! And Mrs. Larsson, please honour them and stay for a cup of tea and some birthday doughnuts."

As they were sipping their tea and choosing their doughnuts, Hannah said, "We can both wear our blue mittens when we go skating together and everyone will think we are twins."

And with that, both girls dissolved into a fit of giggles.

· Chapter 32 ·

By the time school dismissed for the Christmas break, Ting had gone skating with Hannah twice. The first time was a disaster. As promised, Hannah had helped Ting lace her skates. Then the girls walked to the ice with the skate guards firmly attached to their blades. Ting was a little wobbly as they walked along but didn't find it too hard.

Just wait until I get out on that ice! I won't wobble then, she thought as they hobbled along.

Ting was right. She no longer wobbled when she stepped onto the ice. She fell. Hard. Right on her rear end.

"Ow!"

She tried to stand up, but when she put one foot out, the other went a different direction and she landed right back on the ice. She looked up at Hannah in dismay.

Hannah just laughed and put a hand down to help Ting up.

"Don't worry. I did the same thing the first time I stepped onto the ice."

The rest of that afternoon was mostly spent the

same way, Hannah helping Ting get back up after she fell down. At the very end, just when Ting thought her legs might have turned into pudding, she started to get the knack. As she pushed with one foot she could feel herself glide along the ice. It wasn't far, but it was definitely a glide. She tentatively pushed with the other foot and went a bit farther.

"That's it!" Hannah called out to her.

The next time went much better. For one thing, Ting now knew she needed to step gingerly onto the ice surface. She worked hard the whole time on gliding along, and by the end of that session her determination had paid off. She fell down only four times. Hannah told her that at her own second time skating she had still been holding on to the boards the whole time, so Ting felt she had made progress. It was such a good feeling to sail along the smooth surface—well, at least it was until she fell!

Ting was both happy and sad when the final bell sounded before the school holidays. She would be happy to have some time off from school. Even though Ting was a very good student and enjoyed school, it was exhausting to be immersed all day in a language that she was not yet fluent in. Every day her vocabulary grew larger, but the effort made Ting's head feel like it might explode.

But she would miss the times when the teacher read aloud to them. They had just reached the part in *Anne of Green Gables* where Gilbert Blythe had called Anne "Carrots" and Anne had sworn to never forgive him.

Ting would also miss not being able to see Hannah over the holidays. Hannah's family was going to Sweden to spend time with relatives and would be away the whole two weeks.

There was also, of course, the problem of Christmas itself. Ting had been right about the tree. There had been no way to persuade her parents to spend money on a dead tree. Mama did, however, manage to find a small string of multicoloured lights at the thrift store to put around the window. The lights brightened up their apartment even on the darkest, wettest days. Ting enjoyed them so much she wished they could leave them up for the whole year.

Ting wanted to get her parents a present, but she had no money to buy anything. Then she thought about the writing paper Mei Yima had given her. She took out a piece and, using her neatest character writing, wrote her parents a poem about Canada.

"Even if my poem isn't any good, at least they will be happy to see me using Chinese," she thought as she diligently worked away on it, one careful character stroke after another.

She looked at her work when she was done and thought it would pass Teacher Huan's inspection, but she wasn't so sure it would pass Teacher Chen's more careful observation. Oh well, Teacher Chen would never see it. Satisfied, she neatly folded it and placed it in an envelope to give to her parents on Christmas Day.

Three days before Christmas Mr. Dabrowski

surprised them by knocking on their apartment door. When he stepped inside, he seemed to fill the place up. Ting wasn't sure which was bigger—his physical size or his laugh. Somehow when Mr. Dabrowski started laughing it made you want to join right in, even if you hadn't been feeling happy the moment before you saw him. And he was wearing a Santa hat, which made him seem even jollier than usual.

"Hello, Shu and Hai." Then he saw Ting sitting over by the window. "Well, hello, Ting. What are you working on over there?"

"Hi, Mr. Dabrowski. I am reading *Little House in the Big Woods*. Laura's ma thought she was petting their brown cow Sukey, but it was a big old bear."

Ting shivered as she thought about what that must have been like. She couldn't even imagine what it would be like to meet up with a bear, never mind petting one by mistake!

"You like cup of tea?" Mama asked in halting English.

"No, thanks for the offer, but I need to get back down to the shop. I just came up to ask if your family would like to spend Christmas with us. Mrs. Dabrowski and I are going to be on our own this year. Both of our kids are spending the day with their in-laws. You would be doing us a favour by keeping us from feeling lonely."

He looked on expectantly while Ting translated the parts her parents couldn't understand. It would be so nice to go to the Dabrowskis' and celebrate a real Canadian Christmas.

"Please, Mama and Baba?" she asked in Chinese. She didn't want Mr. Dabrowski to hear her begging her parents.

"We have very little to take to contribute, nor do we have any gifts to give."

"But you heard what he said. We would be helping them by keeping them from being lonely. Please can we go?"

Her parents looked at each other, considering her words. Then Baba spoke.

"You can tell Mr. Dabrowski that yes, we would be pleased to spend Christmas with them."

Ting could hardly contain her excitement as she told Mr. Dabrowski that they would be able to come. A time was agreed upon, and after giving them his home address, Mr. Dabrowski hurried out the door saying he had to get back to his shop because they were short-staffed.

The next day Mama hurried Ting out the door in the morning to go shopping. This time, instead of going to the small local shops, they got on a bus and headed to a place Mama said was called Chinatown.

"What do you mean, Chinatown? What is that?"

Ting didn't understand. How could there be a Chinese town here in Canada? And if there was a Chinese town, why was this the first time she had heard of such a place?

"It is a small section of Vancouver with Chinese shops. There are many items from home that I can find there and nowhere else," said Mama.

"Why haven't you told me about this place?"

"I only came here for the first time two weeks ago to get the ingredients for your birthday meal. It costs money to take the bus there, and I can walk to our neighbourhood stores for free."

They got off the bus and walked the short distance to Chinatown. When they arrived, Ting stood and stared, taking in the sights and smells.

"It feels just like home!"

As they walked up and down the sidewalk, going in and out of shops that looked as if they might have what Mama needed, Ting realized it *was* like home, but at the same time it wasn't. For one thing, there weren't just Chinese people shopping. Ting tried to imagine what she would have thought back in Jinan if they had walked down their street to the market stalls and seen groups of Westerners shopping along with them.

Perhaps the biggest difference, though, was the language. The Chinese being spoken here sounded just like that man's on the first day of school—the one Mama said spoke Cantonese. Still, it was nice to see Chinese characters everywhere she looked, and she could read many of them. Some she had learned just recently. *Maybe those boring Saturday classes are not totally worthless*, she thought.

"What exactly are you looking for, Mama?"

"We cannot show up at the Dabrowskis' empty-handed. I thought I would make some pork dumplings to take for Christmas Day. There is a meat seller here who has the perfect ground pork, and another store that has very nice spring onions."

When they walked by one small store that had some baked items and other desserts in the window, Mama told her to just stand there on the sidewalk and wait.

"I'll only be a minute, and the shop looks crowded."

Ting looked inside and didn't notice that many people, but she didn't argue with her mama. She was getting a little tired of shopping anyway. Soon enough Mama was standing beside her again, and they wound their way along the busy sidewalks to catch the bus that would take them home.

• Chapter 33 •

When Ting woke up on Christmas morning, the first thing she did was run to the window and look outside. Disappointed, she turned away. She had checked several books out from the library about Christmas, and in each one there was snow. Ting was used to snow in the winter in Jinan and had been missing the fresh whiteness that made everything look so clean and bright. She had been told it didn't snow very often in Vancouver, but she'd thought maybe since it was Christmas at least a few flakes might fall from the sky. Instead it was rain. Again.

She cheered up when she thought about going to the Dabrowskis' later that morning. Mr. Dabrowski had said to come around ten because Mrs. Dabrowski wanted to show Mama how to cook a turkey. Ting thought of the delicious leftover turkey and cranberry sauce Mr. Dabrowski had brought over after Thanksgiving. These Canadians sure seemed to like turkey! She wondered if they ate it at every holiday.

Mama was already awake when Ting got up. She had been up for hours making the special pork dumplings to take to the Dabrowskis'. It was a lot of work to make the dumplings. First there was the dough. It had to be mixed using just the right amount of flour. Too much, and the dough would not roll out thinly enough. Too little, and the dough would stick to the counter. Then there was the pork filling to be made. It involved getting just the right amount of spring onions, soy sauce, and other ingredients mixed in with the meat.

After the dough and filling were ready, Mama took a small wooden rolling pin and worked on the dough. First she sprinkled some flour on the counter. Then she took a small ball of dough and placed it on the floured surface. Next came the hard part—rolling out the dough so it was paper thin. Once that was accomplished, a plop of meat filling was added and the dough was quickly rolled over on itself to make a neat little dumpling shape.

This process had to be repeated for each dumpling, which is why Mama had gotten up so early that morning. Finally, when all the dumplings were formed, she threw them into a big pot of boiling water and cooked them. They smelled so good that Ting did not know how she would be able to wait until dinner at the Dabrowskis' to eat one!

After Mama finished cooking all the dumplings, she called Ting to the kitchen table. Baba was sitting there with a big grin on his face.

"Merry Christmas, Ting Ting!" he said, handing a small paper bag to her.

Ting was taken completely by surprise! She had not expected a present from her parents, even though she had written the poem to give to them as a gift. She reached into the bag and felt her fingers touch something sticky. Slowly she pulled out two sticks with bright red blobs on them.

"Hawthorn candy!" she exclaimed. "How were you able to get this here?"

Then she remembered her mama's instructions a few days ago to stay on the sidewalk while she went into the sweets shop.

"That day in Chinatown!"

Smiling, Mama nodded her head. Ting thanked her parents with a big hug.

"Just a minute," she called out as she ran to where she had her poem hidden. "This is for you and Baba," she said, handing the envelope to Mama.

Mama carefully opened the envelope and pulled out the paper inside.

Home 我家

I came to Canada 我到了加拿大，
And I missed our happy home. 却惦记着幸福的家。
The smells of the market, 还有市场的气味，
The walks in the park, 公园的幽径，
And my grandfather's face. 祖父的脸庞。
I was scared of this new place. 我惧怕这新地方。

But Canada was nice to us. 可加拿大真好。
I met new friends, 我结识了新朋友，
Played new sports, 迷上了新体育，
Ate sweet doughnut treats. 还尝到甜甜圈。

My new home isn't scary. 新的家、不可怕。
I have nothing to fear. 没有什么值得怕。
Home is there 我的家，就在这儿。
And home is here. 我家就在这儿。

"It's a poem about Canada but written in Chinese. I made it up myself. I used my best character writing," Ting pointed out.

"I can see that," said Mama.

When Mama had finished reading the poem out loud, both she and Baba wiped tears from their faces.

"It is a beautiful poem, Ting Ting," Baba said. "Thank you."

Mama went back into the kitchen to arrange the dumplings on a platter. Ting went to sit by the window and slowly ate one of her hawthorn berry treats. She kept glancing out the window to see if the clouds would clear so she could catch a glimpse of her beloved mountains. She had just finished her candy when Baba called out that it was time for them to go. There was still no sign of the mountains, but Ting was so happy from having eaten the candy that for once she didn't really care.

• • •

The minute they walked into the Dabrowskis' small home, they were inundated with wonderful smells. There were cooking smells coming from the kitchen, mixed with a scent Ting couldn't quite identify coming from the living room.

"Come in, come in. Merry Christmas! I'm Mary Dabrowski."

Mrs. Dabrowski was wiping her hands on her apron as she spoke. Ting saw she had a smudge of flour on her cheek, and from the looks of the apron, it was a good thing she was wearing it or her clothes would have been a mess. Mr. Dabrowski came down the stairs wishing everyone a Merry Christmas, shaking hands and laughing that infectious belly laugh.

Mama had hardly had a chance to take off her coat and respond with her own introductions when Mrs. Dabrowski handed her one of her aprons. Then, in a no-nonsense way, she turned to her husband.

"We have work to do. You men go visit in the living room. I'm sure there is some sporting event you can keep busy with. If you come pester us in the kitchen, we will put you straight to work. Ting, you come with us. I'll need your help translating."

What followed was a combination cooking, language, and life lesson. Mrs. Dabrowski showed Mama how to make the stuffing. Then she showed her how to prepare the bird by taking out the giblets and salting the cavity. Ting's job extended beyond translator— Mrs. Dabrowski called her over to help Mama put the stuffing in the bird. It seemed funny to be shoving seasoned bread crumbs into a bird, and when Mrs. Dabrowski turned the bird around and had them stuff the rear end, all three of them got the giggles.

Once the turkey was in the oven, they were given a lesson in pie making. Mrs. Dabrowski was surprised to see that her student did a nicer job of rolling out the pie crust than the teacher. Mama smiled and pointed at the pork dumplings.

"Much practice," she said.

Mrs. Dabrowski opened the can of pumpkin to make the filling. Ting thought about the can they had taken out of the Salvation Army hamper at Thanksgiving. They'd had no idea what to do with it so had simply tried eating it straight from the can. They'd each taken one bite and no more. It was horrible! Now Ting watched as eggs, milk, sugar, and spices were all blended with the pumpkin. Then it was poured into the pie shell and the pie was slipped into the oven next to the turkey. This looked *much* more promising than eating it straight from the can.

Next Mrs. Dabrowski pulled out a bag of cranberries. Just seeing the round red berries was enough to make Ting's mouth pucker up. She remembered simply popping one in her mouth and biting into it after the Salvation Army man had left them some. Her whole face had puckered up so much, she thought her cheeks might stay permanently stuck to her teeth. Of course, when Mr. Dabrowski brought over the Thanksgiving leftovers, they had learned that you didn't just eat the berries raw. They needed to be cooked and to have some kind of sweetener added. The cooked sauce had made Ting's mouth pucker up a little bit, but in a good way, just like hawthorn berries did.

While Mrs. Dabrowski gave Mama cooking lessons, she told them about her family. She and her husband had come to Canada as immigrants twenty years ago, when their two children were very young.

"It was a difficult time for us. We didn't know anyone, we had no money, we spoke very poor English, and we didn't know if we would ever be able to see the family we left behind in Poland again. Many nights I cried myself to sleep."

Ting thought about how much that sounded like their experience. She listened as Mrs. Dabrowski continued.

"If it hadn't been for the kindness of perfect strangers, we would never have made it. We would have starved. Several different church groups took us under their wing and brought food and clothing to our door, always, it seemed, when we were most in need."

"But now you have a house, and Mr. Dabrowski has the doughnut shop. Things are okay," said Ting.

"Yes, things did turn out just fine, but that doesn't mean it was ever easy. Of course, our children learned to speak English very quickly, but for us it took several years before we started to feel comfortable with our new language. Even now we sometimes struggle to find the right word."

"How did you get the doughnut shop?"

"Well, Peter—" Here she stopped, seeing the look of confusion on Ting's face. "Peter is Mr. Dabrowski's first name. Peter finally found a job cleaning office buildings at night. For ten years he worked at that job, and we saved every extra penny we could manage. All that time he dreamed of opening a bakery here in his new country. You see, he had been a baker back in Poland and loved his work. He noticed that Canadians love doughnuts, so when we finally had enough saved he rented a small space and opened a shop. The business grew until finally there was enough money to buy a place of his own."

"Dabrowski's Donuts!" said Ting.

"Yes. Now we need to check that pie," Mrs. Dabrowski said, back to her no-nonsense tone of voice.

Ting knew Mama was paying close attention to Mrs. Dabrowski's story. She had "that look" on her face—the one that meant she was really concentrating. And she kept interrupting and asking Ting to translate words she didn't understand.

Once the food preparations were complete, Mrs. Dabrowski gave Ting and Mama each a glass of a delicious drink called eggnog, and they joined the men in the living room. As soon as they entered the room, Ting realized what that other wonderful smell was, the smell she had first noticed when they entered the house. It was the Christmas tree!

Set in a corner of the room, it stood so tall it almost touched the ceiling. In fact, it had a gold star at the very top that actually *was* touching the ceiling. There were multicoloured lights strung around the tree, and some were blinking off and on. Decorations of all sizes and shapes were hung on the branches, and under the tree were beautifully wrapped packages. Ting giggled and clapped her hands in delight. Even Mama seemed to be impressed by the sight, judging by the look on her face when they entered the room.

Hmm, now maybe next year we will be able to get a tree, Ting thought.

The rest of the day was full of fun and surprises and delicious food. They all laughed when Mr. Dabrowski produced five sets of chopsticks and handed a pair to each person.

"I thought we would put a new twist on the traditional Christmas dinner," he said, then let loose with his booming laugh.

The food was *all* wonderful, but there was one thing Ting liked more than all the rest put together.

"Mmm," she said when the first bite of pumpkin pie went into her mouth. "Much better than eating it out of the can!"

They all had a good laugh as the story of the can at Thanksgiving was told. Mr. and Mrs. Dabrowski seemed to like the pork dumplings as much as Ting liked her pumpkin pie. Mrs. Dabrowski finally told Mr. Dabrowski he'd better stop eating them or he would end up being more stuffed than the turkey.

After dinner, the men did the dishes while the women went upstairs. Mrs. Dabrowski said she had something she wanted to show them. They followed her into a small bedroom. There was a large wooden chest in the corner. Mrs. Dabrowski opened it and pulled out a photo album. They all sat on the bed while she turned the pages and showed them pictures from their old home in Poland. Suddenly the Poland pictures stopped, and the rest were all from Canada. Ting looked at the bare room in the background of the pictures from when the Dabrowskis had first arrived and thought how much it looked like their own apartment. They were just finishing when they heard Mr. Dabrowski shout up the stairs.

"Should we open the presents all by ourselves down here?"

"We'll be right down, Peter. Patience, please!"

Once they were in the living room again, Ting and her parents sat down and watched in confusion as Mr. Dabrowski reached under the tree and started handing packages out to everyone.

"But we have nothing for you," Baba said. Ting could see by the look on his face and Mama's that they felt terrible.

"Nonsense," boomed Mr. Dabrowski. "You have given us the best gift of all. You have given us the gift of friendship. If you hadn't joined us, Mary and I would have spent the day alone feeling sorry for ourselves. This is our way of saying thank you."

Mama opened her package first. She smiled as she pulled out a bright green apron that Mrs. Dabrowski had made for her. When Mama held it up, Ting could see it had two large white pockets with strawberries embroidered on them.

After Mama thanked Mrs. Dabrowski, it was Ting's turn to open a gift. Her eyes opened wide when she was handed a large package. She carefully pulled paper decorated with candy canes away to reveal a brand new backpack. It was bright blue and had two compartments at the front and several at the sides.

"Look inside!" said Mr. Dabrowski.

He seemed almost as excited as Ting. She reached

inside and pulled out a brand new insulated lunch bag in the same colour blue as the backpack, along with a plastic drink container.

Ting threw her arms around Mr. Dabrowski and said thank you, and then she gave Mrs. Dabrowski a hug as well.

He must have noticed my beat-up old backpack from the thrift store, Ting thought. *But I wonder how he knew about my old paper lunch bags?*

Finally it was Baba's turn. His package was quite small, and judging from the way Baba held it, it didn't weigh very much either. They all watched as Baba opened his gift. Inside the box was a doughnut. Just one doughnut. It was plain, without any frosting or decorations. It didn't even have sugar sprinkled on the top. Baba smiled and said a polite thank you to Mr. Dabrowski. Then Mr. Dabrowski let out his biggest laugh yet.

"Sorry about that doughnut. We sold so many doughnuts yesterday that by the time I remembered to take one out to give you today, this was all that was left."

"It is fine. I am sure it is good doughnut," Baba said. Ting was pleased at how much his English was improving.

"It isn't really a doughnut," Mr. Dabrowski said.

Baba clearly looked confused now.

"Well, it *is* a doughnut, but that isn't really what the gift is meant to be. What I would like to give you is the offer of a job at my doughnut shop. I know you are trained as an engineer, and hopefully you will soon be able to use your skills to get a good job. But until then, well, I am short of workers and you are short of a job. It seems like a good solution for both of us."

When Ting went to bed that night, she had so many thoughts running through her mind that she wasn't sure which thought to think first. In the end she decided on the two most important ones. First, Baba finally had a job. And second, Mrs. Dabrowski's family photo album hadn't stopped in their old country. It had continued right on after they moved to Canada, with many more happy memories filling the pages. Ting was determined to have her album do the same.

• Chapter 34 •

The next month seemed to drag on forever. One cold, rainy day followed another until Ting was sure she would never see her mountains again. Not only that, she caught a nasty flu bug that was going around her school and had to stay home for three long days. She was so sick that even being confined to the lumpy old couch for days didn't give her the trapped feeling she usually got when she spent too much time cooped up in the apartment.

When she was finally well enough to go back to school, she was disappointed to find out that Mrs. McBride had finished reading the last chapters of *Anne of Green Gables*. Ting knew she could check the book out of the library and read it for herself, but it just wouldn't be the same as hearing it read so smoothly to her.

There were some things to be happy about during that long January, though. Baba had started working in the doughnut shop the first week of the month, and he seemed much happier now that he had a job. Mama, too, was happier now that she had made some inquiries at the refugee society about nighttime cleaning jobs.

They also no longer had to have the same old food day after day, so Ting's lunches contained items other than rice, apples, and eggs. Mama went once a week to Chinatown to buy specialty ingredients.

Ting was now doing quite well on her skates. She could keep up with Hannah if they were going forward. She still needed to do some work on skating backwards, but that was coming along. She was sure that by the end of January she would have that skill mastered as well.

Wouldn't Junjie be surprised to see me skating? I would like to see him step out on the ice for the first time!

The thought made Ting smile. But it also reminded her of the letter they had recently received telling them Yeye was very sick. He was making a slow recovery but would need to be in the hospital at least another three weeks. In China, hospital patients were expected to have family members who would provide meals and basic care for the sick person. It wasn't like Canada, where nurses and other hospital workers did these jobs. Between the medication and the other things that were needed, it was costly. Ting had heard her parents discussing it, and they had agreed that they would send some money back to China to help with the costs. Her parents both said how fortunate it was that Mr. Dabrowski had hired Baba to work in his shop. Ting hoped Yeye would be all right.

On the last day of January there was exciting news at school. Mrs. McBride announced that in three weeks there would be an opportunity for interested students to attend a live theatre production of *Anne of Green Gables*. She had chosen this particular show because the class had enjoyed hearing the story so much.

Perfect! thought Ting. *Now I can find out what happened in the part I missed.*

She and Hannah started talking excitedly about the show, wondering what the book might be like made into a play. They had no idea what kind of actor might play Gilbert's part, but they knew for certain the girl who played Anne would have to have flaming red hair. Ting was so excited about seeing the play that she ran most of the way home. She couldn't wait to tell Mama!

"Mama! Guess what? Our class is going to see a play in a theatre. It's called *Anne of Green Gables*. Remember the book I told you about, the one about the girl with red hair? The play is the same story as the book."

"Whoa. Slow down," said Mama. "And please pick up your backpack."

Ting looked down at her feet. She hadn't even noticed she had dropped it on the floor.

"When is your class going to the play?"

"In three weeks, on a Friday afternoon."

Mama's eyebrows shot up at this news.

"You'll miss school for this play?"

"Yes, all the information is here in this note Mrs. McBride sent home from school."

Then, realizing Mama might have trouble reading the note, Ting grabbed it back and quickly read it out to her.

Anne of Green Gables
Friday, February 23
1:00 p.m.
Gateway Theatre, Richmond, B.C.
Cost: $20.00 per student

"I'm sorry, Ting Ting, but there is no way we can afford to pay twenty dollars for this ticket."

"But Mama, everyone else from my class will be going. If I don't go, I'll have to stay back at the library all by myself! And remember, I had to miss the end of the story because I was home sick. This way I can find out what happened."

Ting looked up at Mama with pleading eyes, but her mother remained steadfast.

"I am sorry, Ting Ting. I know you would like to go to this play, but there is no way we can spend the money."

"But Mama, Baba has a job now and things are better. Surely we can find the money."

"Yes, Baba has a job now, and we are thankful for that. But this job does not pay a high salary and we still must watch our money very closely, especially since we are sending money back to China to pay the doctors to treat Yeye."

"But Mama!"

Ting's voice was growing louder and more desperate with each word she spoke. Tears started to flow down her cheeks and she brushed them away angrily.

"Ting Ting, I wish we had the money to send you to this show, but we don't. Someday things will be easier here and such things will be possible. But not this time."

Ting could see that her mama was starting to cry, too, but she was too upset to care.

"Stop calling me Ting Ting. It's a baby name and I'm not a baby anymore. And things will never be better here," she shouted. "I hate it here! I want to go home to China."

For the rest of that afternoon and evening, Ting sat in her chair staring out the window, first at the rain coming down in sheets outside, then at the street lights that came on one by one. Sometimes she stood and watched the buses go by, crowded with people, and the cars that wove in and out of the lanes below.

Mama could not get her to come to the table and eat her dinner. Baba finally told Mama to give up, but Ting could hear the concern in his voice, too. The minutes each seemed to last an hour, but finally it was bedtime. Ting put on her pajamas and despondently crawled under the blankets, pulling them up over her head in an effort to block out not just the light, but also the events of the day.

Of course it didn't work. The harder she squeezed her eyes shut, the more awake she became. The ugly words she had said to Mama swirled around in her head, over and over again. She noticed that her pillow was wet, and it was only then that she realized she had been crying. She felt as miserable on the inside as all the people she had seen walking in the downpour had looked on the outside.

It was sometime later that she heard Baba speak to Mama in a low voice, the voice he used when he was trying to keep from waking Ting. Of course, she was already awake, so she was able to hear every word.

"Shu, this is all my fault. If I hadn't come to Canada on that scholarship, none of this would have happened. We would still be in Jinan. You would be working at the hospital, I would be working as an engineer or teaching at the university, and Ting Ting would not have been forced to leave her home, her family, and her friends. We would not have these struggles."

"Hai, you know you had no way of knowing what would happen. Nobody did."

"That's true, but I still feel responsible."

"Do you think we should consider what Mei suggested?"

At this, Ting's ears worked extra hard.

"Until today I would have said no, that Ting Ting's future would be better if we stayed here in Canada. She'd be terribly far behind in school now in China, and even if she did make it to university, her working life would be much more difficult and stressful there. But now, after this..."

"I have thought the same as you, Hai, that even if it is difficult for us here, we are doing what is best for Ting Ting. Now I am not so sure."

"Well, Mei has said that she does not think there is

any danger now in returning to China, that we can return if we want to."

"What do you think, Hai? What is best for Ting Ting?"

"I think it is best that we go back to China. I had hoped that she was adjusting to life here in Canada, but it appears that is not the case. I'll let Peter know in the morning that he will have to find someone else to help him at the doughnut shop, once we save up enough for our flights home."

For the first time in her life, Ting did not care if her parents knew she was eavesdropping. She jumped off the couch and ran to the table in such a hurry that she didn't even notice she was still holding on to her precious blanket.

"No!" she shouted. The force of her exclamation surprised her as much as it did her parents. "*This* is my home now. I want to stay here in Canada." It wasn't until Ting actually heard the words come out of her mouth that she realized they were true.

Mama and Baba looked at each other in surprise, then at Ting. Without a word, Mama put her hand on Ting's shoulder and walked her back to the couch. Their voices became much quieter after that, but it wouldn't have mattered if they had been shouting. Ting was crying too hard to hear them.

· Chapter 35 ·

Three big things happened the next day. The first thing happened in the afternoon when Ting went to get the mail, a chore she usually disliked. It meant walking down the long, smelly hall to the mailboxes, then standing there trying to get the bent-up old key to fit in the slot. Today it took five tries before she could get the door to open. She sighed as she reached in, thinking it would be the usual sale flyers advertising things they had no money to buy. Instead her fingers landed on an envelope. She quickly pulled it out, and as soon as she saw the sender, she smiled for the first time that day.

Ting burst in the door of their apartment, the letter held out in front of her. "Mama, Baba, look! It's a letter from Yeye!"

Baba took the letter out of her hands, opened it, and began reading.

Dear Family,
I hope you are all well. Thank you so much for the money you sent to help me when I was sick. I am better now and am even able to go to the park with my birds.

Please tell Ting Ting I have a new bird I take with me.
She is a creamy-white colour just like the stick candy Ting
Ting loves so much, so I have decided to call her Sticky.
I can tell from the letter Ting Ting sent that she likes
it very much in her new country. I hope someday it will
be possible for me to come visit and see these mountains of
hers, and watch this game she calls hockey. I hope she is
adding pictures of these new things to the picture album.

Yeye

The next thing happened just an hour after the excitement of getting the letter. There was a loud noise—so loud and surprising it made Ting jump. The noise happened again, and this time Ting realized what it was. Just last week they had had a phone installed in their apartment, and this was their very first call. She felt a little nervous as she went to answer it.

By the time the phone call ended, her anxious look had been replaced by a smile every bit as big as the one she had worn when she discovered the letter from Yeye in the mailbox.

"Who was it, Ting Ting?" Mama asked.

"That was Mrs. McBride. She wanted me to know she had just received notice of the winners of the writing contest our class entered. My poem about Canada—the one I gave you for Christmas—won first place!"

"Ting Ting, that's wonderful," Baba said. "What an honour!"

"She also said there is a prize of fifty dollars for the

first-place entry! When I come to school on Monday she will give it to me."

"Fifty dollars! That is a lot of money, Ting Ting. You can start a savings account at the bank," Mama suggested.

"That is a good idea, but I have a better idea," Baba said. "I think Ting should start a savings account, but I also think she should go on her class trip to see *Anne of Green Gables*. What do you think, Shu?"

Ting could not believe her ears when she heard Mama agree with Baba. Now she and Hannah could go to the play together, and she would get to see the part of the story she missed.

That evening after dinner Ting thought about what a wonderful day it had been. She knew she should feel perfectly happy after the good things that had happened, but there was still a sadness inside of her every time she thought of what she had heard last night. As she slowly wiped the dinner dishes dry, she tried to think of a way to change Mama's and Baba's minds about moving back to China. It was after her fourth sigh that the third big thing that day happened.

"Ting Ting, you need to hurry up and finish drying those dishes. You don't want to be late."

Ting looked over at Baba. He and Mama both had funny looks on their faces, the kind of look grown-ups have when they know something you don't.

"Late for what, Baba?"

"The hockey game on TV. At work today I heard people talking about a big game tonight between

Vancouver and Calgary. If Vancouver wins, they will be in first place in their division."

Confused, Ting said, "I didn't know you liked hockey, Baba."

"Well, I've decided that if we are going to make this country our home, it's time I learn more about this game Canadians like so much."

Ting was so surprised she almost dropped the bowl she was holding. "Really, Baba? Do you mean we get to stay?"

"Mama and I talked about it after you fell asleep last night—really fell asleep, not pretended to. It seems you're very happy here, and your happiness is what is most important to us. It isn't easy for us here. The language is difficult for your mama and me to learn, and it might be a long time before we can find jobs that pay very much money. But we can see that Canada is a good place for you, a place with a bright future. We think this is where you belong."

As they sat together on the old couch listening to "O Canada" being sung before the game, Ting's heart felt happier than it had in many months. This was her home, her place of belonging. And as she joined in and sang the words to Canada's song with the man on TV, she thought to herself, *Now it's my song, too.*